THE KETTLE CHRONICLES:

THE BLACK DOG OF BONGAY

Stephen Morgan

Copyright © 2021 Stephen Morgan

The moral right of the author has been asserted.

Apart from any fair dealing for the purposes of research or private study, or criticism or review, as permitted under the Copyright, Designs and Patents Act 1988, this publication may only be reproduced, stored or transmitted, in any form or by any means, with the prior permission in writing of the publishers, or in the case of reprographic reproduction in accordance with the terms of licences issued by the Copyright Licensing Agency. Enquiries concerning reproduction outside those terms should be sent to the publishers.

Matador
9 Priory Business Park,
Wistow Road, Kibworth Beauchamp,
Leicestershire. LE8 0RX
Tel: 0116 279 2299
Email: books@troubador.co.uk
Web: www.troubador.co.uk/matador
Twitter: @matadorbooks

ISBN 978 1800461 208

British Library Cataloguing in Publication Data.
A catalogue record for this book is available from the British Library.

Printed and bound in the UK by TJ Books LTD, Padstow, Cornwall
Typeset in 11pt Minion Pro by Troubador Publishing Ltd, Leicester, UK

Matador is an imprint of Troubador Publishing Ltd

MIX
Paper from responsible sources
FSC® C013056

Author's Note

John Kettle was one of the first writers to publish works on English Dialects in the late Elizabethan period. It was during research into his work that I came across a box of his unpublished papers, which took the form of a daily journal kept from 1570 until 1592. The following story is based upon John Kettle's journal for 1577...

ONE

The dog stopped at the top of the hill and looked back, his tongue lolling from his great red mouth. There was shouting and yelling in the field behind him, as the men drew near again. The chase had gone on all day, and the dog was now in a land quite new to him. He snarled at the pursuing mob, his red eyes blazing, and loped off down the steep hill.

When the men reached the summit, they could see the dark shape in the vale below, running towards a smaller, flatter hill in the bend of the river.

The dog reached the riverbank. He hated water. There was river ahead, river to the right and left, and behind him he could hear the men crashing through the bushes. He raised his huge, shaggy head to the setting sun, and howled; long, loud and ragged, a sound that slowed the men in their tracks and sent cold shivers down their spines. When the bravest of them emerged into the clearing by the riverbank, there was no dog to be seen anywhere. Instead, chewing contentedly on some roots, was the most enormous black pig the men had ever seen…

But all that was a very long time ago. So long ago, in fact, that no one can recall exactly when it was, or what happened next, or why anyone bothered to remember such a thing in the first place. Don't let it bother you now. Enjoy this beautiful walled garden. It's a lovely sunny day in early September. Sit down on this rustic bench near the herbs. Let the scents of mint and dill and rosemary drift by you in the gentle breeze.

Don't mind the fellow on the other end of the bench. He is part of the story. No, he is not in fancy dress. He is dressed as any other soldier of rank would be in the year 1577. He has that slight frown creasing his brow because he's wondering what he's doing here. Here, is the fine city of Norwich, by the way, and the garden is the walled part of the garden of the Bishop's Palace. It is only a few hundred yards from the noise and bustle and smell of the heart of England's second city, but in its peace and tranquillity, it could be in another world.

The bishop will be along in a minute or two. He has said twelve o'clock and he never allows himself to be early or late for anything. The soldier stands, and walks slowly up one of the paved paths to the sundial. It wants about two minutes of twelve o'clock. He's of about average height, for the time, and has a kindly face with well-regulated features, which becomes almost handsome when he smiles. The ladies in Bear Street say he looks altogether too nice to be a soldier, although they don't say it quite like that, and how would they know anyway? His one distinguishing feature is his hair, which is red. Not "ginger" red, nor carroty red, but a deep, lustrous shade of amber. With the sun shining full on it, like today, it seems to have a life of its own, with its own hints, highlights and solar flares. The aforementioned ladies call him Captain Coppernob, but never to his face.

'Good day, Richard, I hope it finds you well.'

Ah, the bishop is here at last. The soldier takes his hand and kisses the proffered ring. We're getting to know a bit more about him now. His name's Richard and he may well be a captain, although the ladies of Bear Street call all sorts of people all sorts of names, so we can't be sure of that yet.

The bishop is tall and thin, with piercing eyes and close-cropped hair. He's dressed very simply, for a bishop, in black robes, as of the old Benedictine order.

'Take a seat, and we will be to business. It concerns matters in Bongay – you know of Bongay?'

By which you will gather that here we have a focussed, no-nonsense monk of a bishop, who thinks austere, angular thoughts, and never wanders off up, what he dismisses as, the leafy lanes of speculation.

'Er...' says Richard.

He did not know of Bongay. He knew of a saying, "Well, I'll go to Bongay," but he'd had no idea it was a real place.

'No, Your Grace.'

'Well, you will know it soon enough. This year there has been nought but strife and un-rest in that town. In April I had cause to dismiss two church reeves of St Mary's for perhaps carrying their puritan zeal to too great a measure – they broke down the rood screen, and that was not the first instance of them breaking images. In August the church was visited by a terrible storm while the people were at service, resulting in the deaths of two of the faithful and apparent great injury to others, and now we have this.'

Bishop Edmund produces a small, grey pamphlet from his robes and places it carefully between them on the bench.

'Author, one Abram Fleming, apparently resident in London. It contains an interesting account of the aforementioned storm, but with the addition of a large, black dog, such as you see before you on the cover, which, according to the author, appeared in the church at the height of the tempest, and was responsible for the deaths and injuries caused that day. This tale is prefaced by a warning that this was of God's judgement, by which you may gather that Mr Fleming's puritan zeal may even exceed that of our rood-breaking reeves. This tract has been passing among the townspeople for the last week or more, and it is said by the vicar that many are now afraid to come to service and prefer to keep within their own doors, and that there is much muttering and fear about supernatural happenings. You come commended to me, Captain Brightwell, as a man of patience, firmness and sagacity, and not of any great fervour one way or…'

So he *is* a real captain, and now we have all of his name: Richard Brightwell.

'My Lord, Bishop—'

'That is of no matter – indeed it is what I require in this case. I need a clear account of what has occurred in this place, so some peace can be restored to the church and the parish. I take it you have no connections in the locality which might compromise or hinder your enquiries?'

'None that I am aware of,' says the good captain. 'Being from the south shires, Hampshire, and come to Norwich by way of the garrison and from London.'

'I wish you to gather an account from as many witnesses of the storm as you may, also those who claim to have seen the apparition.'

At which point he picks up the pamphlet by one corner, as if it might bite him or give him the plague.

'There are some in here who claim to have seen the beast. Here, take and read it! Also speak to the vicar and the reeves, oh, and to Lady Sherborne, who was the prioress many years ago. Although she is ancient her mind is still extremely active. I have taken the liberty of already requesting your leave of absence from your garrison commander, and I would like you to embark upon this undertaking as soon as you are able. I have made rooms available for you at The Fleece Inn in the middle of Bongay town, both for your accommodation and for those who will travel with you.'

Richard is both impressed and mystified, as he has not yet had a thought about who might be accompanying him.

'There will be your servant of course,' says the bishop, 'and you will need a scribe to record testimonies and to keep notes, and as these are troubled times, I would feel easier if – please do not misunderstand me captain – you took someone who would both be responsible for your own safety, and able to add force to your requests for assistance and enlightenment.'

'My servant is Humfry, and I can take one of the garrison scriveners, John Kettle, but—'

'In this instance I may be able to assist you,' says the bishop. He stands up, produces a small hand bell from his sleeve, and rings it vigorously. When a servant appears the bishop sends him to fetch Augustyn from the refectory.

'Augustyn was my servant for some time at Wymondham Abbey. He has a discerning mind hidden away in his brute of a body, and is the kindliest and gentlest of creatures, except when taken in his cups, or when he fancies an injustice has been visited upon those dear to him. Then he is capable of great wrath and extreme mayhem. He has often served me well, but as Norwich is relatively peaceful at present, I feel he may be more use to you in this undertaking.'

Captain Brightwell sits with his hands in his lap, staring mutely at the sundial during this brief dissection of Augustyn's character. With some men, it is said, you can look at them and it is difficult to know what it is they are thinking. The bishop begins to wonder if he may have been mistaken in Captain Brightwell. He does not appear, at this moment, to be capable of thinking at all. But what does our Lord Bishop know? He had asked, in the highest circles he knew, which were some of the highest in the kingdom, for someone of intelligence and authority, with some wisdom and discernment, and who was not a priest. And he had been sent this rather lumpen looking individual, who seemed to have drifted off into a world of his own, centred on the bishops' sundial.

We do not have long to wait – here is the servant, returning with Augustyn. Augustyn may have been the biggest man Captain Brightwell has ever seen. He's about thirty years old and, in a former age, he would have been a creature of myth and legend, an ogre or a giant. And yet he is not fat, green or ill-favoured. It is as if the Creator set out to make an ordinary man but felt expansive and generous that day. Thus, Augustyn is well over seven feet tall.

'This is Augustyn,' says the bishop.

Richard shakes his hand and finds his own enveloped to the wrist. Yet the handshake is firm, dry and brief.

'How do you do?' says Richard.

'I should have said before,' says the bishop, 'Augustyn has been mute since birth. His hearing is quite unimpaired, and there is nothing wrong with his mind. There is just one other matter. While still a heated youth, in an effort to control his temper, Augustyn took a solemn vow of non-violence. This he has adhered to ever since, and would not feel able to break, under any circumstances.'

'Excuse me, my Lord Bishop,' says Richard, becoming almost animated, 'but what would be the good of a bodyguard and enforcer who refuses to fight anyone?'

'Well, first there is the matter of his sheer physical presence,' says the bishop, 'which I think would deter all but the most foolhardy of miscreants; and second,

Augustyn undertook in his vow not to *offer* violence to any man, but there was nothing, as I recall, about refusing to defend himself, or, by extension, those about him.'

The bishop rings his hand bell again, and a servant appears with a tray, goblets and wine.

As he walks up Tombland in the evening sunshine, ignoring the beggars and politely declining the whores, the captain ponders as to whether this is the next great step forward in his military career. An investigation into the possible existence of spectral dogs in a small East Anglian town? Perhaps not. His servant Humfry, does not seem to think so.

'It's 'ardly the front line, is it, sir? Bunch of interbred bleedin' yokels mitherin' on about some bleedin' bloody dog!'

Humfry was from London, but that is no excuse for his language, which is made up almost entirely of expletives.

'An' that preacher down in London, who wasn't even bleedin' there when it 'appened. What does he bleedin' know?'

'Humfry, be quiet, and please stop cursing. How do you know any of this?'

'Stands to reason, Cap'n. You said jus' now we're going to Bongay, and I was in The Adam n' Eve last night, and the landlord was reading bits of this Fleming's story about a Black Dog in Bongay, and I'd never heard of the bleedin' place 'til then, beg' pardon, and there can't be two of 'em, can there?'

This was before they had even returned to the castle. Richard wonders if the bishop knows that the Black Dog story was already common currency in the taverns of his own cathedral city. As soon as he reaches his lodging, Humfry is sent to fetch John Kettle, while the captain settles down to read Abram Fleming's pamphlet.

'Look on the bright side,' says Humfry, as he and John Kettle make their way through the castle gate, 'there'll be no copying for a few weeks, an' it'll get you out of 'ere.'

'There is that,' says John, 'but where on earth is Bongay?'

'S'not far! 'bout nine leagues south of Norwich. They got streets and stone buildings and the like, the captain says, and the natives speak English, after a fashion, and there's an alehouse round every corner!'

Humfry does not know whether any of this is true, but it sounds well, and he is trying his best to dispel the lugubrious air of gloom that hung around Master Kettle like a marsh mist as they trudged up the hill.

'I used to have a dog, once,' says John.

'Not like this one, you never did,' says Humfry. 'This one's as big as an 'ouse, an' black as night with flames for breff, and burnin' red coals for eyes.'

Or so the landlord of The Adam and Eve had said, when reading from the pamphlet.

'My dog died,' says John.

'Wot jolly larks,' mutters Humfry, leading the clerk up the stairs of the lodgings.

'In agony,' says John.

'I'll leave you 'ere,' says Humfry at the top of the stairway, 'so you can regale the good cap'n with your sunny smiles and funny stories. Tell 'im I have gone to load up the wagon an' prepare the 'orses for tomorrow.'

Richard knew just what he was getting with John Kettle. A fine, dry mind, and perhaps the neatest and clearest script in all the eastern and southern shires, with no blots, mis-spellings or irregular punctuation, but coupled with the most serious mien in the entire kingdom.

'It will be necessary for me to interview a good number of the townspeople,' says Richard. 'I wish you to write down everything that is said, so that the bishop can be presented with a full record of our proceedings. Are you at all familiar with the way of speech in that part of the world?'

'Here in Norwich, yes,' says John, 'but there are likely to be significant variations over what we might consider to be a very short distance.'

'So…?' says Richard.

'But nothing that ought to be below our understanding,' says John, politely, as he meant below *his* understanding.

It is later that evening. Captain Brightwell, although we know him well enough by now to call him Richard, is dozing fitfully in front of his fire, having dismissed John Kettle. The pamphlet still lies half-read upon his lap, and he dreams of dogs and muffled thunder and cracked bells. John Kettle is almost sprightly in his steps back to the castle. He is some way through writing his own *Dictionary of English Dialects*, and this new undertaking may be of great assistance. Humfry is making his way along the outer wall of the Close, towards The Adam and Eve, where tonight *he* will hold centre stage, as one who is to visit the lair of the Black Dog on the morrow.

And Augustyn? He is already in his cell, fast asleep. The bishop has told him he is to go with the kind-looking captain tomorrow and look after him, and whoever and whatever accompanies him. Augustyn could not be said to be dreaming, because life rolls by him in one continuous colourful stream, whether waking or sleeping, but he went to sleep imagining what sort of place Bongay could be, and there are towers, and walls, and a shining river, and a green meadow, and a gnarled old tree in the meadow, and – snuffling and grunting among the tree roots, there is an enormous black pig…

TWO

It's the following day in the nearby village of Poringland. All right, it doesn't look much like a village, just a dusty crossroads with a few scattered hovels and a wayside inn. The road to the west leads to a former roman settlement, so of course it is straight and true. The road south is to Bongay, and the northern road is to Norwich. The road east leads to – somewhere east of here, and as no one in this story is going that way, at least for now, it need not concern us. If you were to stand at the centre of the crossroads at this particular time of day – it's about eleven o'clock in the morning, screw up your eyes and look northwards, you would see a number of dark dots growing larger on the ribbon-white road. If you were listening as well as looking, you would hear vague murmurings coming from the large clump of bushes on your left.

'One of 'em is on an 'orse,' says one bush.

'And there are two more walking,' says another bush.

'And they are leading another 'orse, pulling a cart,' says the first bush.

'The one on the 'orse looks like a soldier,' says a third bush.

'So what?' says the first bush. 'There's only three of them and there's -'s'pose, seven, no eight, no – eleven of us!'

'What we going to do?' says the second bush.

'They reach the crossroads,' says the first bush, 'we rush them, five in front, six behind, swords out: "Yield or die, hand over all your particulars!" Berate the servant with the flat of your swords, 'prehend the wagon and repair to Caister. Scatter in the wood, meet up in Trowse tonight. Hush – they're 'ere! Thomas, remember your words!'

'How now!' cries Humfry (for it was he, sitting atop the wagon). 'What's this apparition, sprung from a bush! What's your business, fellow?'

'Er,' says Thomas, shaking twigs from his hair, 'what day is it today, pray?'

'Wednesday,' says Humfry, 'as you would well know if you had not been sleeping in a bleedin' bush all the morning!'

''Tis also Holy Cross Day and I see neither you nor the dark fellow is wearing a woollen cap?'

The captain has on his head this morning a voluminous wide-brimmed hat beneath which Thomas could barely make out his features, let alone whether he was wearing a woollen cap.

'You are forfeit under the law,' says Thomas; here he pauses and counts on his fingers. 'Six and eightpence, and if he has not a cap' – nodding towards the captain, and raising a few more fingers – 'ten shillings!'

'And who are you to be enforcing the law?' says Humfry. 'The local Justice? I think not, judging by your mode of dress and days of beard! I think you may be less of a law officer and more of a footpad!'

Thomas sighs. He is a man of action, not words. He soon wearies of asking what others are wearing and why. He wants to rob, and if necessary, kill, and he's heard quite enough of this bumptious underling to want to berate him now with the sharp side of his sword. His hand itches for his hilt.

'Let's not quibble over ten shillings,' he says. 'Just give us all you 'ave, right now! You brought nothing into the world, and I'm going to make bleedin' sure you take nothing out of it, neither!'

'Either,' murmurs John Kettle.

As Thomas is speaking, several ill-favoured heavily armed men swarm out of the bushes and surround the three travellers and their wagon.

'What's in the cart?' says Thomas.

'Four travelling bags…' begins Humfry.

Thomas counts on his fingers again. 'There's only three of you!' he says.

'Oh, and a sleeping giant,' says Humfry. 'A rib-cracking, eyeball-gouging, skull-splintering, ball-crushing—'

'Humfry!' says the captain.

'Beg pardon, Cap'n,' says Humfry. 'Give his leg a shake, Master Kettle, if you please!'

John Kettle gingerly waggles one of the two enormous boots protruding from the back of the wagon. There's a surprised grunt and Augustyn sits up, staring wildly about him.

'Ah, good morning!' says Humfry. 'Enjoy your nap? These gentlemen wish to inspect our wagon, so would you kindly step out for a few moments?'

Augustyn climbs off the wagon, and stands up, straightening his tunic and brushing off leaves. The heavily armed ill-favoured men give a collective gasp and back off one pace.

'Yes, he's big, ain't he?' says Humfry. 'But harmless, I assure you. He's taken a vow of non-violence, except—'

As soon as these words are out of his mouth, three of the ruffians leap forward with a rope and try to pinion Augustyn's arms to his side.

'I wish you'd let me finish!' says Humfry, as one ruffian is slammed into a tree trunk and a second somersaults through the air and bounces once off the back of the cart before landing face down in the dirt.

'Except, of course, in defence of those dear to him or the bishop!'

There is a pause now while we all look up, as Augustyn, with a flick of his right arm, launches the third footpad in a vertical direction.

'Well, I've never seen that before!' says Humfry, shading his eyes to get a better view of the flailing, receding dot.

'Now!' he says, addressing Thomas. 'What was it you wished to know about our cart?'

Thomas's reply is drowned out by the crash of his descending companion into a nearby tree, but is something along the lines of, 'I think we'll now be going.'

And with that, they turn and flee, back down the road towards the ancient Roman settlement.

The inn near the crossroads where this event occurred was for three hundred years afterwards called "The Flying Man", until one day a hare was caught by some hounds and ripped to pieces outside the front door. This was observed by the landlord, who promptly re-named his inn "The Hare and Hounds".

The rest of the journey is quite uneventful, and by mid-afternoon they have reached another crossroads, this time in the hamlet of Ditchingham, just to the north of Bongay. To the left lies the road to the coast, and to the right, inland to Diss and Bury St Edmunds. In the middle of this crossroads there is a large grassy mound. Swarming around this mound and onto the road is what John Kettle describes in his day journal as "an inordinate number of domestick fowl". And not any old chickens, pecking and clucking peacefully in the dirt, such as you might encounter in any good-wife's backyard, but big, belligerent-looking birds, many more cockerels than hens, high-stepping in the dusty road, and refusing to move aside from the captain's horse and the wagon.

'Our lodgings are at The Fleece in the main street,' says the captain to John Kettle.

'I'm to visit Lady Sherborne at Ditchingham. I hope to join you for supper.'

He reins in his horse and trots off in a nor' nor'- east direction. We shall stay with John Kettle for the nonce, as an interesting confrontation with a massed phalanx of poultry is about to occur. The bravest of the cockerels are already pecking at the ankles of the wagon horse, and he, though normally a phlegmatic beast, is beginning to snort and shake his head, and show signs of irritation.

'Be off, chickens!' yells Humfry, from the wagon seat. 'Master Kettle, how are we to remove these birds?'

Even as he speaks, there is a loud, long "cluck!" from the far side of the mound, followed by, 'Eeaarrr, my neat brown 'ens, eeaarrr, my fine black cocks, eeaarrr, my lov'ly chucks!'

The serried ranks of chickens turn as one and hurry off behind the mound.

'Wait here!' says John Kettle to Humfry.

We'll go with John, because there's no immediate danger, and we might learn something.

On the other side of the mound there is a small man with a wooden handcart, from which he is tossing handfuls of seed to the clamorous circle of chickens about him. It takes John Kettle some time to attract his attention, because of the racket, and because John has not a loud carrying voice, and is a shy man, and loath to shout, or even wave his arms about.

After a few moments of "ahems" and "excuse me!" the man turns his head in John's direction long enough to note his presence. The man raises an arm and moves towards him, and the sea of chickens flow forward and surge around John Kettle's ankles.

'Good day to you?' says the man. 'Don't mind them!'

He gestures to the hens pecking close to John Kettle's feet.

'They are peaceable birds – enough! Is your business in the town, or on The Way?'

John Kettle divines from this that the road from Diss to Yarmouth is known hereabouts as "The Way". He said his business was in the town, without saying what it was, or who was with him, but that he would be glad of a safe passage through the chickens, and directions to The Fleece Inn. And are these chickens his, and if so, what are they doing here on the highway?

The man replies that they're not his chickens, and indeed belong to no man, but have, as far as anyone knows, always been here. Folk hereabouts said that, before the time of the Romans, there was once a farm at this crossing, which had been long abandoned, but the chickens had stayed on, even when it had again become a road heavy with travellers. He feeds the chickens every day because nobody else does. He offers John Kettle his hand.

'Mellchioedech Foweler, as you find me! That's with five "e"s!'

'That is a name with a Biblical ring,' says John Kettle. 'Are you perchance after Melchizedek, from the book of Hebrews?'

'Very likely so!' says Mellchioedech. 'Although there's a deal of spelling got in the way since then! If you would like to call your companions I will direct you to The Fleece. I only ask a small toll in passing, it goes nowhere but the chandler's pocket to buy more feed for these birds?'

John Kettle is fascinated by Mellchioedech Foweler's name and his manner of speech. The first thing that strikes Humfry, upon circling the mound, is the size of his ears. Mellchioedech is a small man, with crinkly brown eyes, a wide grin, and ears that stretch from his temples to halfway down his jawbone. Humfry cannot take his eyes off them.

'Well, if that flying fellow back yonder had such ears as those, he would have floated back down in spirals, like a fevver,' he mutters to Augustyn, oblivious and asleep in the wagon-bed. They walk over the river bridge and up the steep hill to the square in the centre of the town.

Captain Brightwell rides through the archway into the courtyard of Sherborn Hall, a fine red-brick manor house. After a few moments' calling a servant girl appears at the open door and escorts him upstairs.

'Just walk in and announce yourself, sir; she will be in her sitting room, but her hearing is as sharp as my fish knife!'

Captain Brightwell proceeds somewhat gingerly along the hall towards an open door on the left. He is not good around furniture and does not wish to upset anything.

'Who is that?' calls a gruff voice from within the room.

'Captain Brightwell, from my Lord, the Bishop of Norwich, to see Lady Sherborne?'

'In here!' says the voice at the far end of the room, in a window bay, on a high-backed chair. She is one hundred years old, the bishop had said, and she can't see very well, and you will have to speak up and clearly, but otherwise you will not find a keener mind in the parish. Lady Sherborne is stick-thin, with a shock of short white hair in a sort of halo around a nut-brown, high-cheek-boned, deeply lined face.

She offers the captain her left hand.

'Excuse the sinister greeting, Captain, my other hand has rather given up on pleasantries. Sit down – there!'

She indicates a chair opposite her.

'Now you won't have to shout at me to make yourself heard,' she says. 'The bishop wrote I was to expect you – you have come to know something of the town, and of the storm, and oh – of our dog? I'm old now, of course, and take no part in the town's business, but the servant girls here are quite frenetic – and keep me well-informed with news and gossip. You must understand that I have not been prioress for these forty years past. But what is it you want to know?'

Richard wants first to know about the rood-breaking reeves of St Mary's.

'Like many churches in these times,' says Lady Sherborne, 'the old ways have gone forever, but as soon as we put on the new, then that is swept away as well. Some in St Mary's would like to hold on to their past, and some see any candle or statue or wall-hanging as an abomination and a return to popery. It is not just a matter of faith; it is politics, jealousy and revenge, laced with a generous measure of ignorance and stupidity. I speak plainly, as there is nothing any man can do to me now.'

Richard also wants to know about the storm on August 4th last.

'It did make the most tremendous din. I have only known one other like in my life, when I was a small girl.

The clouds brewed above here to the north for an hour or more, and I was in the garden and had to be brought in when the rain began. It was as dark as a November night. The church tower was struck by lightning it is said, and John Fuller and Adam Walker died there.'

Richard wants to know about the Black Dog.

Lady Sherborne laughs wheezily and shakes her walking stick.

'Of that I can tell you but little,' she says. 'Throughout August, you could not find a soul in Bongay who had any knowledge of a dog, cat or donkey being anywhere near the church on that Sunday, but then, when this appears,' she picks up a copy of the Fleming pamphlet, 'it seems that many of our good folk did see the hound after all, and were indeed savaged by it.'

Richard couldn't help but notice that she had said "our dog" earlier.

'Oh yes, that!' She laughs again. 'Well of course, the Reverend Fleming may be unaware of it, but some would say we have had dogs here for many centuries. Indeed, there is an old tale that the black dog was here before the town. And that the Bigods at the castle had a ghost dog at their command, and a mad friar from this town had a dog which possessed his spirit. And that the beast appears from nowhere at many places in the vicinity, and is often a harbinger of death or misfortune, and can take whatever form it pleases.'

'Er – I thank you,' says Richard. He had come hoping the aged prioress would have given him some useful background knowledge of the town, and she has, but this has now been somewhat overlaid with flashes of lightning, an elusive, shape-changing hound, and skeins of local myth and legend.

'You look very low for someone who has come for succour,' says Lady Sherborne. 'Listen to the townsfolk, but do not believe more than half of what they tell you, because they will only say what they think you want to hear! And on no account tell Mrs B what Mrs A has been saying about it; or she will tell you the exact opposite as a point of principle.'

Richard rises to take his leave and takes Lady Sherborne by the left hand.

'One more thing,' she says, 'there are a few simple-looking people wandering the lanes of this town; more than you may be used to. Give them as good a hearing as those you suppose to be in their senses. Good day to you, Captain! My steward will show you out.'

Lady Sherborne's steward is Bernard, a man with an open weather-beaten face, a wide smile and a deep musical voice that seems always on the verge of laughter.

'A remarkable woman, Lady Sherborne,' says Richard.

'Oh – ah!' says Bernard, beaming like the sun in the morning.

'Have I said something to amuse you?' says the captain.

'Ah – oh, no – I don't think so!' says Bernard, with an even broader grin. 'She is, as you say, a remarkable lady. Very wise and sagacious, but then she has lived a powerful long time, mostly half as long again as most hereabouts, so you would doubtless pick up a little wisdom here and there along the way?'

'You were not among those at the service?' says the captain.

'Oh – ah – no,' says Bernard. 'If you're meaning that where the dog was to have appeared, I was in attendance here as usual to her lady.'

'Lady Sherborne spoke of other black dogs in the town, of a legend going back past the time of the Bigods. You have lived here all your life, have you ever seen or heard anything of these apparitions?'

Bernard puts his hand on his heart and gazes on the captain in mock sorrow.

'I'm afraid I must disappoint you.'

At this point the huge grin breaks out again.

'I was once witness, as a small boy, to a black cat jumping into a bucket, which tipped over and deposited the unfortunate grimalkin into the well below, where he used up all of his nine lives at once; but as to a large canine apparition, I am pleased to say, especially as they are rumoured to be harbingers of death and destruction, that I have never set eyes on one.'

The captain is learning quickly that even quite brief questions to Bernard produce answers of great longevity and complexity.

'Er – thank you!' he says.

'Which does not mean,' goes on Bernard, 'that you would find me walking the lanes of the South Elmhams alone after dark. Who knows what you might see scampering across the fields towards you! Take the lane to the left of the church, cross the bridge and go up the hill into town. The Fleece is on the other side of the market place, opposite St Mary's. Good day to you, sir! Oh – and my wife has seen him!'

He says this so abruptly that Captain Brightwell, in the act of mounting his horse, slips through his stirrup.

'Not in the church you understand, but when a small girl she was down the back of Castle Hill, walking up to the town to get her mother some milk, when that appeared out of the Swan yard, big as an 'orse, she said, looked at her with the red eyes, and then passed on. She backed up against the wall, said that smelt right rank – said she felt cold and clammy and sweaty, like when you've eaten a bad pickled egg that starts rising up. And that was the Black Dog and all, and no other, because not a week later her grandmother upped and died!'

'How old was her grandmother?' says the captain.

'Eighty-five,' says Bernard, 'but she'd never had a day's illness all her life 'til then.'

Richard mounts his horse and turns towards the manor gate.

'I'll perhaps want to talk to your wife at some stage,' he says, 'her name?'

'Mistress Susan Curdye,' says Bernard. 'Although I warn thee, she usually does most of the talking. I'm the quiet one of the family!'

The captain is back at the crossing. The chickens are nowhere to be seen. As he rides around the mound he spots something moving in the undergrowth. A dark shape flows across a space between two bushes. Richard reins in his horse and waits. After about half a minute, the tips of two black ears appear from a bush. They turn slightly left, and right, and back in the captain's direction. As he trots slowly towards the town side of the mound the ears follow his movements. They disappear briefly and resurface behind another bush. Captain Brightwell does not pretend to know much about the natural world, but he thinks he knows a hop when he sees one.

'The Black Rabbit of Bongay!' he murmurs as he turns his horse towards the town.

THREE

Bridge Street, the road into Bongay from the north, ascends a steep hill, and John Kettle and his small company are nearly at the top when they are accosted by two men lounging on a small scruffy green outside an alehouse.

'Look, Nick – that's a travelling show!' says one of the men. 'Come on, give us a turn, boys! Whaddya do? Juggling, something funny with yon giant?'

The road is too steep to stop and start a horse and cart when climbing, so Humfry contents himself with a wish to further their acquaintance in the taproom of The Fleece Inn, although he doubts whether such elevated personages as they can frequent such an establishment.

The man called Nick looks a bit baffled and scratches his head, unsure whether he's being complimented or insulted, so he offers the observation that they had better be here on honest business, that's all, or Mr Belwood will have something to say about that. Humfry withers him with a look and urges the horse up the last few feet to the town square.

'At least as honest as any you would be involved in.'

The Fleece is a large rambling, rickety edifice, with many outside stairs which lead to other outside stairs or landings with locked doors. It's halfway down the High Street, exactly opposite St Mary's Church. The taproom is a warren of nooks and settles, with two large fireplaces. And here is mine host. No, not him, that's Mr Josiah Kindred, here for a meeting upstairs of the feoffees and the town reeve. The landlord is the small personage filling pewter tankards three-in-a-hand from that large barrel over there, a Mr Moses Mellendyne, shaped not unlike a small barrel himself, but sharp of eye and short with speech.

'Good day to you, gentlemen!' says Master Mellendyne, as he weaves between Humfry and Augustyn, six foaming tankards held aloft. 'Assuming you are gentlemen, and thus welcome here. Are you expected?'

Having delivered his ale to one of the fireside tables, Mr Mellendyne returns, wiping his hands on his apron.

'I believe you are,' he says before they could answer. 'I have had a letter from Norwich about that!'

He says this last part in a very loud voice, so that everyone in the inn could hear, and looks about him fiercely, as if to challenge anyone one else who has had a letter from Norwich to speak up quickly, or hold his peace.

'That spoke chiefly of your tall friend and his accommodation. Perhaps he had better sit down, before his head goes through the ceiling, and he joins the meeting upstairs! He is a man of few words, as I understand?'

'He is a man of no words,' says John Kettle. 'He is a mute.'

'Well, begging his pardon for that,' says Moses, 'but I'm sure he'd still make more sense than any of them up there!'

By this we can gather that Mr Mellendyne has no great opinion of the feoffees, and wouldn't become one even if he was asked to. He has never been asked to, but he's not about to say so, and anyway, he can't stand about here gossiping, he has an inn to run, and was there not a captain, a military gentleman, among you?

'He will be with us shortly,' says John Kettle. 'I understand you have kindly set aside a room for our business?'

Mr Mellendyne has indeed set aside just such a room, but that is at present occupied by the fortnightly meeting of the town reeve and feoffees aforementioned, and he will be pleased to show Mr Kettle, and the captain if he has finished his other business and is present, as soon as the reeve has finished his business. In the meantime, after seeing their rooms, would he and his companions take some ale?

They sit in a corner by the street window. On the journey down from Norwich Richard had instructed them not to gossip with the townsfolk as to the purpose of their visit.

'Which makes it a little difficult,' says Humfry, 'when 'im over there says, "Wot's yer business?" I can't up and say, "We're 'ere to see if you've all bin seeing things and are out of your wits," now, can I?'

'This is a small place, and they will all know by tomorrow anyway,' says John Kettle, 'once they have read the handbills.'

Humfry has put up a number of handbills throughout the town inviting those who had been at the service on August 4th or had witnessed anything unusual to assemble in The Fleece Yard at nine o'clock tomorrow morning.

'Ah, look here, Nick!' says a sneering voice. 'That's the Poringland Giant again, and his two little dwarfish friends.'

Humfry puts his tankard down on the table.

'Do you know, Master Kettle, I had a high opinion of Mr Mellendyne until just this moment, but it does seem he will let just anyone frequent his inn.'

'So, when's he going to do some tricks for us?' says the man called Nick in a loud voice. 'No point in 'aving a freak for show if he doesn't show, eh lads?'

'I've already had to explain this once today,' says Humfry wearily. 'He is not a freak, he is a mute, who has taken a vow never to offer violence to any man.'

'Is that so?' says Nick, leaning over the back of the settle and slapping Augustyn twice on the cheek. The room falls silent. Nick is not known for his bravery, and is no more stupid than the next man, but it is a public holiday today, and he has been drinking since not long after he got up. The room holds its breath. Augustyn doesn't appear to notice he has been slapped and continues to gaze out of the window at the fading silhouette of St Mary's church tower.

'Well, I believe you're right in what you say, little dwarf,' says Nick, giving Augustyn another slap. 'Now out o' there, that's our cubby'ole in that corner, so we can see what's what outside. So shift yourselves!'

Humfry declines to move, and Nick takes hold of his jerkin, only to have a large hand close over his and prise each finger away. The hand transfers itself to his collar, another grabs him by the britches, and Nick finds himself off the floor, swinging back and forth in an alarming manner. Humfry opens the door of the inn, and points out into the night, and Nick is launched into the great outdoors.

'He said something,' says John Kettle, 'as he sailed past you, I thought he said something?'

'He said,' says Humfry, '"I thought you said?" but I didn't catch the rest!'

Captain Brightwell is just about to turn into the stable yard when the inn door onto the street opens and a man flies out, narrowly missing his horse. The man gets up, cursing mutes, dwarves, dogs and dragons, notices the captain, and asks him what the devil he thinks he's looking at? He is too impatient for an answer, and storms off down the street.

FOUR

It's a bright, rain-washed September morning, and here is Miss Cicely Kindred, walking briskly up Bridge Street to buy some bread and some milk in the Market Square. She notices a handbill pinned to the wall of The Chequers Inn, and several others fluttering from the corner of market stalls. Cicely recalls her father was waving one around when he returned from his meeting last night. He was complaining about it, but she hadn't really been listening, as he was always complaining about something. Here's another one, posted on the wall by the baker's door. Going to buy bread on a fine morning was no chore, there was the wonderful smell from the oven, the warm loaf in her basket back down the hill, the looking forward to "break-fast", that was better than breaking fast itself. There is a small queue, so Miss Kindred has ample time to read the handbill. It says it is "An Invitation", but it reads more like a summons. "All those, who were present at the Divine Service on the morning of August 4th, to gather in the yard of The Fleece Inn, at nine o'clock, to hear a message from the Lord Bishop."

It becomes clear to Miss Kindred what her father had been moaning about last night. He'd said he was damned if he was going to walk back up the hill in the morning just on a bishop's say-so, and Mrs Kindred had said she did not like to hear profanities and bishops in the same sentence, and profanities not at all, not in her house, and anyway, if he recalled, he had not been at the service on August 4th, because he had complained of the gout, doubtless through taking so much wine on the evening before in The Chequers, which, she reminded him, was nearly as far up the hill as the church, although she never had heard him complain of the rigours of that particular journey!

This verbal cannonade had effectively silenced Mr Kindred, who retired to his chamber forthwith. Miss Kindred remembers being at the service, indeed it was so unlike every other church service she had attended, that she felt she was never likely to forget it. She reads the handbill once more, and decides she will attend the meeting, if only to point out to the author that he has not made it clear whether the bishop or just his message will be present.

Mr Josiah Kindred does not want her to attend, but Cicely gently but firmly points out to him that she was at the service in question, and he was not. She also reminds him that while she has a duty to him as her father, her first duty is to God, as she is being reminded every Sunday and Holy Day, and every day in her prayers, and the bishop is after all, a bishop, representing a higher power, so she doesn't see how she can very well not go?

Mr Kindred, who has now been bested in argument by both his wife and daughter in the space of twelve hours, retires to his chamber again to read his journals and pamphlets, where he may express his opinions of them forcibly and freely, safe in the knowledge that they will not rise up from his lap and assail him with rational arguments and plain common sense.

At five minutes before nine, Miss Kindred ascends the hill and crosses the square to The Fleece Yard, which she finds overflowing with people. Miss Anna Poope, Cicely's friend since childhood, is among this throng, and she guides them to a small space by the yard wall, from where they have a clear view of the balcony.

'I do not recall this many people in church at Christmas,' says Anna, 'never mind a stormy Sunday in August!'

'But there have not been many Sundays in this town when the church is struck by a thunderbolt, two men lose their lives and a ghostly apparition is said to appear!'

'Very likely so,' says Anna. 'I expect some of these here have just come to gawp. I doubt if Nicholas Vyner or Simon Costerden over there have been in a church by law since they were baptised – if they were ever baptised!'

'Sooth, Anna! That is nearly blasphemous!'

Miss Poope does not care a fig and tosses her red hair to indicate as much. Anna is a bit of a free thinker, or at least free enough for a place such as Bongay. She sometimes listens to the Reverend Smythe's sermons on a Sunday all the way through and can even talk about them intelligently afterwards.

'Well, they have already fallen foul of the bishop's men, and one of them was thrown out of the front door of The Fleece just last night!'

Anna is the niece of Moses Mellendyne, and has called upon her uncle already this morning, so knows all there is to know about the visitors from Norwich and the events of yesterday. Thus, she is able to name the four men standing on the balcony with her uncle, who is trying to hush the crowd.

'The giant is called Augustyn, he is a mute, and acts as their protector I believe, I'm not sure about the two in the middle, one is a servant and one a secretary; I do not recall their names, or even if uncle told me them, and the other one is Captain Richard Brightwell – he's quite a fine-looking man, do you not think?'

'I saw him this morning,' says Cicely. She had walked back through the churchyard from the baker's shop and had passed behind a man standing before the church porch looking up at the blackened tower. He had caught the scent of new-baked bread from her basket and had looked over his shoulder. Their eyes met briefly and he had murmured "good day" before returning to his scrutiny of the tower.

Mr Mellendyne has succeeded in quieting the throng and makes a half-joke about not realising the level of piety in the town, before introducing the captain, who has a message to deliver from the Bishop in Norwich.

The captain speaks well and clearly; the bishop has been very concerned at recent events in Bongay, especially at the deaths of two parishioners at a Sunday service, and the rumours of a supernatural presence on the same day, and he has sent Captain Brightwell to talk to as many who attended the service and are willing and able to do so, and then report back to the bishop. The captain's servant and secretary will be moving among you collecting names, and a list of times and names will be posted on the door of The Fleece and in the Market Square later today, and the testimonies will commence at nine o'clock tomorrow in the upper room of The Fleece Inn.

'Are we going to go?' says Anna.

'I wonder what we shall say,' says Cicely. 'It was so dark that day, I can hardly be said to have seen anything!'

But there will be an opportunity to speak for a few minutes to someone from outside the closed circle of family and friends and acquaintances in Bongay, so they don't spend more than a few seconds thinking about it before pushing gently through the crowd until they find themselves near enough to Humfry to give him their names.

'Miss Cicely, with no "s"s, Kindred wiv' no "a"s and Miss Poope with two "o"s, like the deck, but with an "e" on the end,' says Humfry. 'An' you'll both be a welcome sight for 'is sore eyes, after seeing some of the old wizens and crows I've been scribblin' down 'ere!'

Humfry's next vision is not so fair, a large, saturnine square man in black, with a down-turned mouth, heavy jowls and cold grey eyes.

'You – yes, you fellow! Write this down! Mr Thomas Belwood. I will see the bishop's man at ten o'clock on the morrow, as I am to London on business in the afternoon. I do not expect to be detained for more than ten minutes, and you may tell your master that I think all this a great waste of time and money, and a possible source of mischief! If the bishop is so interested in our affairs in Bongay, it is a great shame that he cannot bring himself rather than send some raggedy captain on half-pay!'

Having delivered himself of these opinions, Mr Belwood strides out of the yard, his lackeys, Vyner and Costerden, clearing a path before him.

It is later that afternoon. Humfry is walking with Augustyn along the riverbank. Richard Brightwell and John Kettle are upstairs in The Fleece.

'There are ninety-four names here,' says John Kettle, 'although the priest insists there were not above fifty in the church that morning.'

'We will see them all,' says Richard. 'I want as many tales as possible to tell the bishop. Where there are husband and wife or friends or families sitting together we will see them as one. It should not take above three days, although tomorrow will be a half-day as Mr Mellendyne tells me there is a great football match in the afternoon, between the two town parishes. And there is to be a play in three days outside the Trinity church. We shall see Mr Belwood at his appointed hour – not through his arrogance, but because he may have much of interest to relate.'

Let's leave the captain and Mr Kettle to their lists and escape into the early evening sunshine. Here are Augustyn and Humfry strolling through the meadow alongside the river.

'Well, Gus,' says Humfry, 'this 'as turned out as meet as it could be, for you and me anyhows! It's about the best brief the captain's ever given us. He and Mister Kettle are in a stuffy room at The Fleece, while we visit every bleedin' inn in the town! Oh – of course, purely to gather the local mind, as it were! An' no more than two cups in every alehouse. An' no more than five alehouses in a day. It's still going to take us a week. Still, someone's got to do it, eh?'

Their first call is at The Falcon Inn, at the bottom of the hill on Bridge Street, two doors down from Josiah Kindred's house. If you're wondering why Mr Kindred walks halfway up the hill to The Chequers rather than use this place, just take a look around at the locals. See what I mean? We'll be all right if we stay close to Augustyn. Humfry sets about "gathering the common mind". He loudly orders some ale for himself and Augustyn, and sits at the most central settle he can find, where he can be seen and heard from most parts of the inn. Producing Abram Fleming's pamphlet from his jerkin, he favours the company with a few extracts, and then expresses his strong opinion. Humfry alternates this opinion inn by inn, as instructed by the captain, so whereas in the taproom of The Wheatsheaf, near The Staithe, he states very decidedly that there was no such thing as a "Black Dog", and never has been; here in The Falcon Inn he is just as determined that the Reverend Fleming is correct in every detail, and describes every hair of the ghostly hound as if he had seen it himself. Humfry promotes some debate and argument by buying ale for all those prepared to express their opinion, but listens as much as he talks, and reports all back to the captain.

There is one very drunken man in The Falcon, who persists in disagreeing with everything Humfry says, and keeps asking him, "What does he know?" although it comes out as "Wassha-knee-no?" He gets up very close to Humfry, grabs his jerkin, and wags a grimy finger in his face.

'Wassha-knee-no? Seen the bliddy dog I have, blacks ash night, and red as bliddy blood 'is eyes, I sheen 'im, I tell you, I knows 'im, yes, I should do, and don't you say no bliddy different, an' I know who sent him!'

Humfry cannot help but notice that the hand gripping his jerkin is short one thumb and forefinger and is about to ask how he came by this interesting injury when Augustyn takes the fellow firmly but gently by the throat, causing him to release his grip and cease all conversation.

'That will do for today,' says Humfry, as they made their way up Bridge Street. 'We've 'ad our stoup of ale, plus what that rough feller 'as just breathed over me, so we'll leave the delights of The Queen and The Chequers for another day.'

John Kettle moves the inkwell two inches to the left, steps back from the table, strokes his chin, and moves it back an inch. He is in the upper room of The Fleece, and it wants about five minutes before nine o'clock, when the day's proceedings will begin. The sun is shining brightly and the room needs no other light. The captain has a desk-table and chair in front of the street window, and John has put a small settle and two chairs in the centre of the room, facing the table. John is sitting at a smaller table in the corner to the left of the captain, where he can both take notes and observe the demeanour of the townsfolk. John Kettle is both nervous and excited – this, after all, is why they have come to this strange little town. For the fifth time he picks up his quills, examines the points and puts them down again. At nine o'clock, the captain nods to John Kettle, takes his seat behind the desk-table, and instructs Humfry to fetch the first of the townspeople.

They are Robert and Goode Abbs, of Broad Street, a retired merchant and his wife. He is small and bald, with a pointed white beard and tufted eyebrows, and she is small and plump, and smiles a lot.

'I do not know of what use we can to you, to be sure,' says Mrs Abbs. 'There was so very little to see, the day being so dark, and we always sit in the pooh near the back of the church, so we are in no throng upon our departure; and then there was a flash – which we were later told—'

'I thought I saw—' begins Mr Abbs.

'—Was lightning,' goes on Mrs Abbs. 'And then that grew darker still, and there were cries and screams from behind us, which they said afterwards was poor Mr Fuller and Mr Walker in the bell tower but I was on my knees of course, praying as hard as I could for that to stop, for by now that was like unto a visitation, so I couldn't see anything even if a good-body could turn around—'

'But I…' tries Mr Abbs again.

'And he saw nothing, either,' says Mrs Abbs, 'Being as he was on his knees right along beside me. There was some more commotion in the aisle, below the altar, but as I understand, and Mrs Newman told me this, she was in the pooh right next to his, that poor unfortunate Stares boy had a fit of his demons right there in the aisle, driven mad by the thunder and the noise and the dark, I'm sure.'

'There are some reports of a black dog being seen in the church,' says Richard.

'Yes!' says Mr Abbs, 'Come to bring the Lord's retribut—'

'Oh, you mean all the piffle in that pamphlet!' says Mrs Abbs. 'There is quite enough nonsense talked in this town without bringing in more from some crackpot preacher from London! No, people were all crazed enough by the thunder and the rain on the roof and the lightning and the darkness without there being no dog as well. And if anyone says different,' here the smile vanishes and Mrs Abbs frowns at the captain, and glares at poor Mr Abbs, who has just opened his mouth again but closes it quickly, 'then that is just fancy talk, and should not be taken note of! Now we have told you all we know, and we are now going to call on Mrs Newman, so if you will kindly excuse us.'

By the time Mrs Abbs has finished this sentence she is already halfway to the door, pushing the hapless Mr Abbs before her, so the captain wishes them both "Good day".

'Well!' says Richard. 'A very decided opinion in favour of an un-aided storm.'

'Although I think Mr Abbs would like to have seen a dog,' says John Kettle, 'had he been allowed.'

'Put a tick by her name and testimony, and a star by his,' says Richard. 'We may speak to him on his own at another time. He seems to fear his wife far more than he could any spectre or apparition.'

'If he can speak on his own,' says John, 'as Mrs Abbs never allows him the luxury of finishing a sentence, I fear our conversation would consist of nothing more than a series of beginnings and no endings!'

'Whom are we to see now?' says Richard.

'Miss Plesance Balles and her companions of that morning, Miss Alice Cocksedge, Miss Annable Jolly and Miss Christian Godly.'

The next half-hour passes very pleasantly for all concerned, as the four young women are both pleasing to look at and engaging in conversation. Although there are four chairs set out for them, one or other is continually rising and walking about as they talk. They are all slightly in awe of the captain, and Annable thinks John Kettle looks a decent sort of man but needs cheering up. Mr Kettle is in fact in quite good spirits, the frown is one of concentration, as he tries to get down on paper the fluttering, disjointed, and sometimes contradictory thoughts of the four friends.

'Well, we hain't been allowed to sit together for too long, being as are we've only been of age this last year,' says Miss Balles, 'and we were up on the left side near the pulpit, so we could hear all of Mr Smythe's sermon.'

'So we could voo Matthew Curdye in profile, more like!' says Miss Cocksedge. 'What a fine clean-looking young man he is!'

'Such pale skin and soft hair,' murmurs Miss Jolly.

'And that leather jerkin he wears,' says Miss Godly, 'and them boots!'

'Such a fine leg, such strong thighs!' sighs Miss Jolly.

'Ladies,' says Richard, 'loath as I am to disturb what is obviously a pleasant recollection—'

'Pardon, Captain,' says Miss Jolly, 'but Plesance is proper crazed about him – she'd sit out on the porch pooh in January if he chose to sit opposite.'

'And he had not spoke for more than above five minutes, Reverence Smythe, that is,' says Plesance, completely ignoring her companions, 'when there were a mighty crack of thunder and all the candles were gutted, and everyone commenced screaming and yelling, and there was a strong smell of burning in the air—'

'There certainly was a great commotion in the aisle,' says Miss Godly, 'but that may have been the poor Stares boy and the melee about him, but we were not standing looking about us by then, we were all hurrying for the porch.'

Richard picks up the Fleming pamphlet.

'Oh, we've heard all that!' says Plesance. 'Too often if you ask me. My Father reads that out every night aloud like that was holy writ. Yet he was not at the service, but is pleased to tell me what that is I have and have not seen!'

'So, what did you see?' says Richard.

'There was something,' says Plesance.

'There was something very amiss there that day,' says Alice.

'I think that was no more than the storm,' says Christian.

'Nor I,' says Annable.

As their amiable chatter fades away down the stairwell, John Kettle is of the opinion that they are quite handsome women for such an out-of-the-way place.

'One of their number seemed to find you quite handsome herself, if I may judge from her constantly glancing in your direction and the brilliant smile she gave you just now.'

John Kettle affects to have noticed no such thing, as he was concentrating on his note-taking, which has revealed, you will not be very surprised to learn, that two of the young women thought they had seen a dog, and the other two were equally sure they had not.

The advent of Mr Thomas Belwood, at ten o'clock, is preceded by a great deal of noise and hubbub from below. It seems that Mr Belwood again feels the need for a path to be cleared for him through the throng, so Mr Vyner and Mr Costerden are quite needlessly shoving and pushing people about who were not in the way in the first place.

They are met at the foot of the stairs by Mr Mellendyne. He is looking fell and grim, and he tells Mr Belwood that he may do as he pleases, within the law, out in the street, but within the confines of this inn he has no power or jurisdiction to order his, Mr Mellendyne's, customers, in or out of his way, and that he can be about his business upstairs, alone, and then depart, as soon as he should like.

Mr Vyner and Mr Costerden protest that they are going nowhere, until Mr Mellendyne indicates with an eyebrow the presence of Augustyn, on a settle by the fireplace, quietly reading a book.

'And before you ask,' says Mr Mellendyne, 'I lent him that and other books last night, and he now regards me as the dearest of friends, so I'd wait outside, if I were you.'

Mr Belwood waves them away and ascends the staircase. It seems he has no time for pleasantries, he is here to tell the story straight, and then that will be an end of it.

'That posturing fool, Smythe, had been drivelling on for more than a half-hour about the love of God for our fellow man, when it is evident to any sane person that what our fellow man needs is some retribution and punishment for his slovenliness, laziness and dirtiness! This was not long in coming, for there appeared amongst the claps of thunder and flashes of lightning, a vast black hound rushing down the centre of the church that leapt upon Adam Fuller and John Walker where they knelt, and wrung their necks in an instant. The beast vaulted another pew and grabbed young Abraham Stares by his back and flung him down in the aisle. It then returned through the church and out the door, raking it with its claws as it passed.'

'Were you not frightened by this creature?' says Richard.

'My conscience is clear,' says Mr Belwood.

'So, you see this apparition as an expression of God's anger?' says Richard.

'How can it be other? It was sent as a warning to the godless people of this place!'

'Surely more than a warning?' says Richard. 'Two men have died, and a boy already crippled has received further terrible injury.'

'Fuller and Walker were well known in the town for slighting the word of God, and the boy must have had great sin in him to be so afflicted.'

'So, you are quite satisfied that it happened just as described by the Reverend Fleming?'

'It was as he wrote it down.'

'But I understand he was not present at the service?' says Richard.

'But those who were have given him a faithful recollection,' says Mr Belwood.

'And does that include yourself?'

'I have met with Mr Fleming,' says Mr Belwood. 'Now I have spent more than enough time answering your questions. If you wish to spend the next few days sitting here hearing the same story over again that is your business, but I must be about mine.'

And without waiting for leave, he is gone.

FIVE

Mr Belwood is gone, and the sun breaks through the clouds, and shines in the windows of the upper room, lightening the countenance of John Kettle, as he corrects his notes.

'A man sure of his own mind, our Mr Belwood,' says John.

'That would be one way of describing him, certainly,' says Richard.

'He seemed very sanguine about the appearance of the dog,' says John, 'yet quite certain as to how Fuller and Walker met their deaths.'

'And that such a death was almost a natural consequence of their being there. I am not sure of Mr Belwood, he seems like a man who, who…'

'Like a man,' says John, 'of whose nature you would think would be among the very last to be concerned with supernatural visions and calamities, and yet appears very determined, even compelled to be so?'

The captain could not have put it better himself, or indeed, so well. He looks at his list. There are two brothers to see together, and then he and John can have their dinner downstairs.

'Do we know anything of these siblings?'

'The brothers Rune,' says John, 'Thomas and Cornelius, born and bred in the town, and said by Mr Mellendyne to be the keepers of its history. He said if I were taking notes to have a sharp quill and a supple arm, as "they talk much and together", as he put it.'

'One other matter before they come, what is this "pooh" we keep hearing of this morning?'

'It is their singular way of saying "pew",' says John Kettle. 'To say "pew" as you or I do, it is necessary to draw the lips back into almost a smile.'

'Pew!' says Richard, grinning inanely.

'Precisely,' says John. 'Whereas, to say "pooh", as is favoured in these parts, you must push the lips forward, as if to use a peashooter.'

'Pooh,' says Richard, pouting like a madam in a Tombland doorway.

'They use the letter "v" in the same manner,' says John, warming to his subject. 'Where you might remark on the prospect or "view" from the top of the church tower, they will speak of the prospect or "voo".'

If John is hoping to add to his list of interesting local dialects, the Rune brothers are something of a disappointment; both being former pupils of Bongay

Grammar School, and carry their learning lightly but well. The school masters have done their job diligently, as there is only the occasional lapse into the locality from Thomas, and none whatsoever from Cornelius. It is evident these two are brothers as they take up chairs before the captain, but they are not too alike, Thomas is solid and square, while Cornelius is thinner and rather languid.

'Were you both at the service?' says Richard.

'I was there…' says Thomas.

'From the beginning,' says Cornelius. 'But I had arrived – when did I arrive?'

'You came just as the Reverend Smythe ascended the pulpit steps,' says Thomas.

'So, a good half hour too early then,' says Cornelius. 'What was his subject?'

'Sin, and forgiveness,' says Thomas, 'which, given what followed…'

'Was either divine inspiration,' says Cornelius.

'Or retribution,' says Thomas.

'Did you see?' begins Richard.

'The great dog? No, I saw nothing during the time I was there like a dog,' says Cornelius. 'Though it was very dark and there was a great deal of noise and excitement in the aisle, so I cannot be *absolutely* certain.'

'No more can I,' says Thomas. 'Although there was *something* there other than just a storm, as I ran for the door I was brushed past by something great and rank and hairy, which fairly knocked me out of my way.'

'Something trying to get out?' says Richard, getting a word in at last.

'No,' says Thomas, 'something trying to get in!'

'It is said hereabouts that you know much of the history of this place,' says Richard. 'Have there been any other events of this nature that you can recall?'

'Well, there's our dog of course – not our dog of Bongay, but the one that haunts all this part of the land,' says Cornelius. 'That we call "Black Shuck", although he is not in the habit of attending divine service – you are more likely to encounter him out on a lonely path at night, or in a back lane, and he is feared as a harbinger of death. No one thought of him until Fleming's pamphlet appeared. Anyway, he's a Shilly-Shally, and may not even have been a dog at that time.'

John Kettle cannot help himself.

'Excuse me, but what is a "Shilly-Shally"?'

'It is a word we use for a creature that may change its shape,' says Cornelius. 'There is an ancient tale that when Black Shuck first came into this country he was pursued by hunters and trapped in our bend of the river, so changed himself into a black pig, and the hunters felt so at home in the place he had brought them to, that they began to settle as farmers, but when the time drew near to kill the pig for the winter, he changed again into a rook and flew away.'

'And,' says Thomas, 'it is said that in the time of the castle, Sir Hugh Bigod captured the creature, and made it by hunger a ravening beast, and would release it into the lanes and streets of the town only on his birthday, and would not take a drink in celebration himself until it had returned with blood on its jaws.'

'Human blood, that is!' says Cornelius. 'But what is so exciting the townspeople now is that the creature had not been seen, until this forth of August, by no man nor child for many years, and that it was beginning to be thought that our dog had left us and would return no more, until this recent happening.'

'And there is another old story,' says Thomas, 'that the Shilly-Shally can be taken and bound while in a benign form, other than a dog, and – I can't recall the rest.'

'What do you know of Mr Thomas Belwood?' says Richard.

The brothers exchange a smile.

'In faith!' says Thomas. 'How swiftly we move from speaking of ghostly apparitions to solid humanity!'

'Though Mr Belwood does have an aura of darkness about him,' says Cornelius. 'He owns many properties in the town, he has a fine house beneath the castle wall, and a farm in the Ilketshalls, and we believe another house in London. He is a feoffee and was the reeve only two years ago. For our part, we think him grasping and avaricious, and too fond of his own way.'

'And very harsh in his judgement of others,' says Thomas.

There are times, when asking questions of others, you may be obliged to ask for information that you know already, in order to prepare the ground for what you hope will be new revelations. Thus the captain begins a series of enquiries as to the relationships between St Mary's and Holy Trinity churches, their priests and wardens, and the local upheavals caused by the many changes over the last twenty years. Some of this is interesting, and concerns our story, but most of it is not, so while the captain and the Rune brothers are ploughing through the uninteresting bits, let us stray outside for a time. Nicholas Vyner and Simon Costerden departed The Fleece at the same time as their master, so peace and tranquillity reign below, with just a gentle murmuring in the taproom where Humfry and Mr Mellendyne are playing a friendly game of dice. Augustyn ducks his head through the front door of the inn, crosses the street, and makes his way through the churchyard to the north porch of St Mary's. Inside the church, a group of four men are standing around a hole in the north wall.

Mr Edmond Denny, the local stonemason, stands back and scratches his head. Today has not been a good day, so far. Mr Belwood has just been in here, fresh from his interview with Captain Brightwell, and not at all in a good humour. He wanted to know, in a very loud voice, why the work he had ordered on the new window in the north wall was not proceeding, and what was he paying Master Denny (and these other wastrels) for? Mr Denny had kept his countenance and tried to explain, in as calm a voice as he could manage, that the reason for the delay was simple. In the place Mr Belwood has chosen for his window, chosen so that it could be seen from the upper rooms of his house by the castle, there has been discovered the top of a pointed stone archway, belonging to a former door or window, long plastered over. The window space is blocked by medieval bricks, and Master Denny, like all masons before and since, was all for plastering over all the lot and beginning the window above, but Mr Belwood had at that time insisted on removing the top six or seven rows of bricks from the arch, and sending a small boy into the hole to see, he said "where it might lead".

Mr Denny is of the firm opinion that Mr Belwood cared not a straw where the window or doorway might lead, but was making certain there were no caskets of jewels or bags of gold concealed there. For, as Mr Denny said to Moses Mellendyne that evening, what is the point of making a secret chamber if it contains no secrets? When the Rune brothers heard of this discovery, they did their best to persuade Mr Belwood to have the opening completely uncovered, so they could learn something of its history, but he would have none of it. He was paying for the work, the installation of a window celebrating his munificence, and he was damned if he was going to be delayed by two penny-pinched clerks and their crackpot interest in the olden days. Mr Belwood had repeated these sentiments in the last half hour and told Denny to recommence the work directly, or he would not see a penny of his contract. It being eleven o'clock, Master Denny and his workmen take themselves to their dinner, passing Augustyn in the doorway.

The interior of St Mary's is a great open space, with no distinction between chancel and nave, flooded with September sunlight through the great west window. Augustyn walks around the whole church until he comes upon the bricked-up arch in the north wall. There is some scaffolding and planks around the hole, but Augustyn is so tall that he can look in easily. What he sees makes him start back in some confusion. He looks into the hole again, walks again around the church, before looking a third time. Augustyn takes a deep breath and strides out of the porch door. A few minutes later he returns, with a somewhat reluctant Humfry in tow.

'What do you mean, you bleedin' great lummock, hauling me away from my dice?' says Humfry. 'I was in a fair way to recovering my losses 'til you turned up!'

Augustyn picks Humfry up and deposits him on the top plank of the scaffolding, where he can see into the archway.

'All right, what's the jest?' says Humfry. 'I may not be big, but I'm too big to climb in there!'

Augustyn shakes his head furiously and growls. He places his forefingers by his eyes and waves them up and down.

'You just want me to look in there?' says Humfry. 'Then why didn't you – oh no, of course, you can't!'

Humfry stares as hard as he can into the dark archway.

'I can see – bleedin' absolutely nothing!' All right, all right, keep your countenance, I'll look again. No, nothing.'

Augustyn lifts him down, none too gently.

'I'm sorry, I'm sure,' says Humfry. 'I know you wanted me to see something, but either it ain't there no more, or it's something only you can see. An' there's no need to sulk.'

Back at The Fleece, in the upper room, the four men are poring over two books. One is the burial register of St Mary's, which Captain Brightwell has borrowed from the vicar, and the other is Abram Fleming's pamphlet.

'If you look at the entry in the register,' says Richard, 'it is clearly written: "John Fuller & Adam Walker slayne in the tempest in the belfry in the tyme of prayer upon the Lord's Day the iiiith of August," and then here in the margin, "The Tempest of Thunder". Yet here on the third page of Fleming's account he says: "This black dog… passed between two persons, as they were kneeling uppon their knees, and occupied in prayer as it seemed, wrung the necks of them bothe at one instant clene backward, in so much that even at a moment where they kneeled, they strangely dyed."'

'In the days that followed the tempest,' says Cornelius, 'it was always understood that they had died in the church tower, and that their bodies were burnt and blackened by the thunderbolt.'

'Though we have not seen their remains,' says Thomas, 'I believe Ellen Peele and some other poor women laid out the bodies, perhaps you may apply to them?'

'Yet there are many who now claim that these two died in the aisle of the church, as Fleming has it,' says Cornelius, 'though some say the beast seized them in its jaws, and flung them about, and others say they died of fright, which would not be so unlikely.'

'There is no means by which the dog – if such there be – could have reached Fuller and Walker in the belfry?' says Richard.

'There is a narrow stone stair to the bell frame,' says Thomas, 'but they were not there, if they were in the tower they would have been in the ringing chamber below, and that can only be reached by a steep wooden ladder. I do not think a dog, even a spectral dog, can climb a ladder.'

'And there is no record, by Fleming or any of the people of the town, of the beast being seen in or near the tower,' says Cornelius.

'From what you knew of Fuller and Walker, can you think of any reason for anyone wanting them dead or harmed?' says Richard.

'They were both feoffees, and had some wealth and clout. They were always very willing to give their unvarnished opinions on any civic matter, so they were certainly not the most popular men in the town,' says Cornelius, 'and they did not altogether hold with this new severity of faith and custom, which is why I would have thought they were content to remain in the bell tower during the service.'

'To see them devoutly kneeling in prayer before the vicar would certainly have been a unique occasion, I'm sure,' says Thomas.

'It is past the dinner hour,' says Richard. 'Gentlemen, I thank you, and may wish to speak with you again.'

The Rune brothers are in a haste to depart, as they are assisting in the preparation for the town football match, to begin in a few hours.

'That goes back here I don't know how long,' says Mr Mellendyne, as he serves John Kettle and the captain their dinner. 'Though we are but a small town we are two parishes, St Mary's and Holy Trinity, and there is a goal set up at the farthest end of each. For St Mary's it is where the end of Broad Street meets The Way, and for Trinity where the Ollands meet.'

'And how is the winner decided?' says John Kettle.

'There are no rules to speak of,' says Moses. 'The first team to score seven snotches, although in some other places they play to nine.'

'Snotches?' says John Kettle. 'What is a "snotch"?'

'That's our way of saying a goal,' says Moses. 'Someone – the reeve usually, is meant to keep a count of the goals, but that generally goes on until that stops. That's good for my business, but the playing can get a little rowdy at times, a few broken arms and heads here and there, the occasional death – you know the sort of thing!'

'Is it not a little – er, illegal?' says John Kettle.

'Oh yes, sir, I believe it is so – in the country at large, certainly,' says Mr Mellendyne, 'but no one takes any mind of what goes on in such a small place as Bongay! I mean, don't get me wrong, gentlemen, we always obey the new laws of the land – we just like a bit o' time to think about 'em!'

Mr Mellendyne is about his business, and the captain and John Kettle are just finishing their dinner and beginning to wonder where Humfry and Augustyn have got to, when they are approached by Mr Foweler and Mr Curdye. They are in The Fleece for ale, but they have a favour to ask. If the captain could spare him, and he was agreeable, would Mr Flowerdew consent to be part of the Holy Trinity team in the forthcoming football match? As they are speaking, Augustyn and Humfry come through the door; and Augustyn readily accepts the offer to play for Holy Trinity. Humfry is looking a little crestfallen.

'In the interests of fair play and good politics on our part,' says Richard, 'perhaps Humfry should line up for St

Mary's – taking care, of course; to avoid any unpleasant confrontation with the opposition, or indeed, members of your own team?'

Humfry is delighted with this arrangement, and immediately commences a number of complicated wagers with all who will deal with him in the inn, concerning the number of goals to be scored, his part in the scoring, and the possible injury to players such as Mr Vyner or Mr Costerden.

There is still half an hour before the game begins, and Augustyn is very eager and insistent that Richard and John Kettle accompany him to St Mary's.

'You had best go and look,' says Humfry, sagely, 'or, even though he cannot speak, we will never hear the end of it!'

John Kettle looks long and hard into the dark archway but can see nothing but stone and shadow. Augustyn sighs deeply and pats him on the shoulder.

'You weren't so sanguine when I saw nothing!' says Humfry.

The captain looks in and sees the dark-lined face of a grim lady, her head draped in a dark cowl. It is on the wall, to the left of the opening, as if she were looking out malevolently on the bright outside world. John Kettle looks again.

'With respect, captain,' he says, 'it is but a trick of the light.'

'With respect, Mr Kettle,' says the captain, 'it is the face of a woman.'

'Well,' says Humfry to Augustyn, 'the captain sees what you see, and Mr Kettle don't see what I don't see, so you can stop being mad at me now, see? Oh, and if you comes across me holding a pig's bladder in a field or a dark alley this afternoon, just remember it's only a game!'

The captain doesn't say much on the way back to The Fleece.

'John, I want you to find Mr Edmond Denny and bring him to me upstairs, if he is not involved with the football.'

Before he goes to his room, Mr Mellendyne informs the captain there are a number of the feoffees waiting on him, concerning the same football game.

A group of four men, all dressed in black, a Mr Dorlett, Mr Towtinge, Mr Grime and Mr Mountell. None of them are smiling. Mr Dorlett gets straight to the point, as there is little time. The football match must be stopped. It is ungodly, it promotes riotousness, violence (if John Kettle had been present he would have marked that Mr Dorlett said this as if it were two words, "vio" and "lence"), drunkenness and vice, and it is but a remnant of the old days, and now has no place. And he goes on to say, and here he makes his big mistake, that Mr Belwood agrees very strongly with these sentiments, and would have expressed them himself, if he had not been absent on other business.

'Is this all of the feoffees?' says the captain.

It is not, says Mr Dorlett, there are also Mr Foxly, Mr Goodwine, Mr Graygoose, Mr Dickersonne, Mr Hemline, Mr Myngey, Mr Kindred and Mr Gallant.

'And are all these gentlemen absent on business?' says Richard.

It seemed they are not, but Mr Dorlett appears reluctant to say where they are. Mr Mountell, a small man with weak, watery eyes, despairs that all of them bar Mr Kindred and Mr Hemline will be searching for a safe place from which to observe the forthcoming match. His three companions glare at him and tell him to hold his peace.

'And Mr Kindred and Mr Hemline?' persists the captain.

'They are at home,' says a sullen Mr Dorlett. 'They would not say for or against the football.'

'I am only a master of simple arithmetick,' says Richard. 'But it seems to me that even if Mr Belwood's strong sentiments had got the better of him, and enabled him to attend this meeting, there would still be fewer feoffees against the football than there are for it?'

'Ah,' sighs Mr Mountell, 'so it was in council!'

This remark earns him another fierce glare from his fellow feoffees.

'I have neither the authority nor the inclination to interfere in the affairs of this town, other than those concerning the recent events in St Mary's, and as it seems you gentlemen are, by your own admission, in a minority in the matter of the football, I can only wish you good day, and a speedy passage to your homes.'

'Mr Belwood shall hear of this!' says Mr Dorlett.

'Give him my compliments,' says Richard, 'and tell him to come himself next time he has a complaint!'

John Kettle is at the door with Mr Denny.

'What business can you have here?' says Mr Dorlett, angrily.

'None but my own, sir,' says Mr Denny, 'and none of yours, as I recall.'

'Why are you not at work on Mr Belwood's window?' says Mr Dorlett.

'That, sadly, is also business only between myself and Mr Belwood,' says Mr Denny calmly, 'but if I did feel the need to offer an explanation to some such as you, I might remark that there is to be a game of football hereabouts, and that I would not therefore be like to expose my men to any mishap or accident. Good day to you, sir, gentlemen!'

Mr Denny turns his back on Mr Dorlett and proceeds up the stairs.

'I cannot think what you want me for, sir,' says Edmond Denny to the captain, when they were seated upstairs. 'I was not at the church on that August Sunday, I was visiting my sister in Beccles.'

The captain does not care for that; he wants to know if Mr Denny was present when the stone archway in the north wall of St Mary's was opened.

'I was there, sir, with Mr Belwood. It was I who removed the top brick,' says Edmund.

'Did anything untoward happen?' says Richard.

'No, sir, there was a small cloud of black dust did puff out, which I thought nothing of, as there may have been a draught from some opening in the outer wall. Some of it caught Mr Belwood in the eyes, and he did a good deal of rubbing and complaining, as if it were my doing – but you have met him and now know what he's like?'

'Yes, indeed,' says Richard, 'and was that all?'

'Well, nearly all,' says Edmund. 'And please don't think me queer, but I did not think the air within was quite right?'

'How so?'

'I would expect a space between two great stone walls to be colder than a January morning,' says Edmund, 'but the air within, when I put my hand there was warm, and there was no rank stench of decay or damp, but – well, you know the scent of a warm bed just left?'

'Yes,' says Richard.

'It smelt just like that. Almost, and this sounds right crazed – as if there had been something living there!'

Richard tries to look as if this is the sort of thing he heard every day, and walks over to the window and gazes out on St Mary's church across the street.

'Have you told anyone else of this?'

'Oh no, sir,' says Mr Denny. 'I do not wish to be thought a clown or a muddle-head – it would not be good for my business!'

'Of course not,' says Richard, 'and what you have told me will be told to no other, you may rest easy.'

SIX

As Richard and John Kettle step out into the street they join what appears to be a vast sea of humanity, moving in a quiet hum of conversation towards the Market Cross.

'There will not be any room for football games,' says John.

'Oh, there will,' says Mr Mellendyne, who has accompanied them. 'As soon as the match begins, these many will disperse to the inns or their homes. It's generally best and safest to view the proceedings from an upstairs street window!'

On the north and south sides of the town square are lined up two large groups of young men, who are waving flags and banners and cat-calling to each other.

'Those on the north side, with the green and yellow

favour, are St Mary's men,' says Moses, 'while these here in the blue and white, are of Holy Trinity parish.'

A thin man in a purple robe and black hat, carrying a scroll under one arm, and a large, round pig's bladder under the other, walks slowly to the centre of the square. The crowd falls silent, except for one youth of St Mary's who continues to liken the young men of Trinity to the hogs in Skinners Meadow, until shushed by his fellows.

The thin man adjusts his hat, places the bladder at his feet, unfurls his scroll, and takes a half minute to clear his throat.

'That is Doctor Gordon,' says Moses. 'The town reeve, who do love the sound of words and their articulation, but takes a powerful long time to say anything. It's said that some of his patients have tooken and died of old age while he was still telling them what ailed them. This may last longer than the match!'

The town reeve says how it is a fine day and how honoured he is to be asked to begin the match, which is such an ancient tradition, so many of which have been lost in the last years, when everything seemed to be changing, and how he hopes the football would be played in the right spirit, and that no one would come to any great harm.

Here, Moses whispers to Richard that perhaps just a little harm would be good for the doctor's business.

Not only does the good doctor articulate every syllable of every word, he also leaves an age at the end of each sentence, so the crowd keep thinking he is done, only for him to start up again suddenly. A number of the young men are growing visibly restless.

The town reeve, having advised the players of the whereabouts of the goal-posts – the southern one at the Olland Gate and the other at the north end of Broad Street – is just beginning a reminiscence of an old man he used to know who lived in Broad Street, when an ancient vegetable, launched from somewhere near the back of the St Mary's team, sails through the air and bounces on the cobbles, landing not far from Doctor Gordon's person.

The reeve pauses in his remarks, and peers at the vegetable, which appears to be some species of venerable turnip.

'That's as fair a warning as can be managed,' breathes Moses. 'Let us hope he takes the hint!'

'Time is pressing on,' says Doctor Gordon, rolling up his scroll and picking up the pig's bladder. 'Are the teams ready for the match to begin?'

There is a great roar of assent from both sides of the square. The doctor flings the bladder over his shoulder high into the air, turns on his heel and runs for his life.

'I would never have thought he could move so quickly,' says John Kettle, as a purple blur shot past them into the doorway of The King's Head.

'Even the good doctor would know this was one time he could not linger,' says Moses. 'Why, there was one town reeve some years back, who tarried long enough to be swept up by the teams, and found himself adjacent to the ball, as it were; and was discovered sitting in a ditch beyond Broad Street an hour later, having "scored" one of the goals. Now, gentlemen, you may do as you wish, but there is food and drink in your room upstairs at The

Fleece, where you can view much of the town in safety from your big window.'

As the pig's bladder falls back to earth, the football teams rush together, and are now locked in a great, heaving scrum in the centre of the square. Occasionally the ball surfaces from this seething, swearing, grunting mass, at which all around jump into the air to catch it, before resuming their subterranean shoving.

'Can you see either Augustyn or Humfry?' says Richard.

'Augustyn is over there,' says John Kettle, 'leaning against the wall of The Three Tuns, and seeming to take no part in the game, as of yet, and Humfry...'

There is an eruption of yelling on the far side of the square, and a small, spare figure, with the ball under his arm, detaches himself from the throng and, cackling dementedly, races off down Cross Street in the direction of the churchyard.

'There is Humfry!' says John Kettle. 'Let us hope he does not live up to his name, and trip, or he is like to be trampled by those great oafs behind him.'

Humfry, the pigskin clutched firmly to his chest, is well aware that a slavering throng of beefy apprentices in blue and white are in hot pursuit, but is sufficiently fleet of foot not to let it worry him. He is more than a third of the way across the vast open space of the churchyard, and can see the Olland Gate in the distance, and is even beginning to think of himself as opening the scoring with a glorious solo goal, when three Trinity men, who have been lying behind a low, grassy mound waiting for precisely this moment, leap out and tackle him, respectively around the chest, waist and legs. Humfry is brought to earth, the pigskin shoots skywards, and he just has enough presence of mind to curl himself into a little ball before the company arrive. A full-scale battle ensues in the middle of the churchyard, a yellow and green tide heaving south, and a blue and white mass pushing northwards. Humfry finds himself enmeshed in a sea of legs, boots and knees until a giant hand grips his arm and pulls him free, sets him on his feet beside the cursing scrum, and gently dusts him down. Augustyn kneels down in front of him, solemnly holds up one enormous finger, then two, then three, and waggles his eyebrows in an enquiring manner.

'One, two, three!' says Humfry 'Thanks, Gus – I'm fine, now get on with the game! Oh – your play, I think!'

The pigskin comes squirting out of the melee into Augustyn's outstretched arms. He looks at the ball, and then down at Humfry, who is vainly trying to wrap himself around one of his massive thighs. Augustyn lifts his leg and shakes it a couple of times, as one might attempt to remove a troublesome beetle, and Humfry flies off into a nearby bush. Augustyn tucks the ball under his arm and strides off purposefully in the direction of the town square.

The scrum has now separated itself, and there is some consternation among the St Mary's contingent.

'The giant has got the ball! We must bring down the giant!'

Another battle begins, as the Trinity men form a protective u-shaped phalanx at Augustyn's rear to ward off the St Mary's team in the churchyard.

Richard and John Kettle are still outside The King's Head when Augustyn comes striding back into the square. He stops and waves to them, an opponent clinging on to his arm like a green and yellow rag doll, before making for the entrance to Broad Street. There he encounters ten men of St Mary's, standing in line across the street, barring his path.

'Now, we mean you no harm, Mr Flowerdew,' says the bravest of the men, 'and 'tis only a game, so if you'll just give us the—'

Augustyn throws the ball high into the air and, as the men turn to mark where it returns to earth, he steps over them, takes five paces up the street, catches the pigskin as it falls, and proceeds up the street to the goal, crossing the line with what seems like half the St Mary's team clinging on to his legs.

'St Mary's, nil – Holy Trinity, er, one!' says the town reeve, very slowly, as the teams file back into the square. Mr Dickersonne, the senior feoffee, restarts the match, but he is not as quick on his feet as Doctor Gordon, and is swept away in the crowd, emerging some time later in Castle Orchard with his robe torn and his ceremonial hat jammed down around his ears.

'I'm not sure that Holy Trinity will have it all their own way this time,' observes John Kettle, as the goal scorer passes by with a nod and a smile, surrounded by about fifteen of the biggest, meanest-looking green and yellow favoured men of the town. 'Augustyn seems to have won himself some attention.'

The St Mary's men are making a determined comeback, and are moving in numbers into the churchyard where they have formed a human wedge with the ball somewhere in the middle. They are advancing slowly but surely in the direction of the Olland Gate. As they can see nothing from the Market Square, Richard and John Kettle return with Mr Mellendyne to the upper room of The Fleece. Richard is beginning to form an opinion about the game of football.

'It is not so much about getting the ball into the goal,' he says, 'as preventing as many of your opponents as possible from getting the ball – by whatever means, fair or foul.'

'It is like war without the weapons,' says John Kettle.

As he speaks, a group of St Mary's men run past towards the Olland Gate. A company from Trinity leap out of Priory Lane and assault them with root vegetables.

'Well, it's like war, anyway,' says John.

Augustyn is trying in vain to reach the St Mary's wedge, but the fifteen men dedicated to stopping him are putting in a valiant effort, and keep returning to the task, despite being regularly picked up and tossed aside like straw in the wind. The wedge reaches the gate, the Trinity goalkeeper is trampled into the mud, and when safely over, the ball is produced and triumphantly placed beyond the goal line. A ragged, exhausted cheer goes up from the St Mary's players.

'It's all right, Gus!' says one of his minders. 'You can stop for now, we have us a snotch!'

Augustyn puts the man he is holding by the throat and groin carefully onto the ground. He grins broadly and shakes each of his erstwhile tormentors warmly by the hand.

'Don't get too friendly,' says the minder. 'It's only one goal apiece – we'll be at you again presently!'

Mr Myngey, the next senior feoffee with the doubtful privilege of restarting the game, employs a different and somewhat unusual tactic. Casting all dignity aside, he sets off at a gallop from the door of The King's Head, holding the pigskin at arm's length in front of him, as if it were about to explode. Upon reaching the centre of the square, he tosses it into the air, shouts, "Begin!" and races off in the direction of Bridge Street. It is quite an effective ploy, if your first idea is self-preservation, and you don't care too much for the dignity of your office, for he clears the clashing front rows of St Mary's and Trinity by a good ten yards, and arrives in safety at the door of The Queen at the opposite side of the square.

Humfry has been getting his breath at The Green Dragon, and has been enjoying his glass of ale and the conversation of the landlord, a Mr William Gildersleeves, so much, that he has missed the restart. The yelling and cursing in the Market Square bring him outside, and, as he makes his way towards the noise, he notices two figures slinking off down Brandy Lane. There is a gust of wind down Broad Street, and Humfry hears a faint humming sound above him. He has only had the one glass of ale, so it cannot be that. There it is again. He looks around him carefully, and then above. Where the street narrows, between the gables of Fleshly's Vintner's on one side and the corner of The Three Tuns on the other; at a height of about seven feet from the ground, a slender hemp rope has been stretched so thin that it is difficult to see anywhere but against the sky.

'Well, I'll be!' sighs Humfry. 'And they say it's only a game!'

Humfry returns to The Green Dragon, borrows a ladder from the obliging Mr Gildersleeves, and returns to the corner of The Three Tuns. He climbs the ladder and cuts through the cords until they are attached only by a single strand but retain the appearance of a sound rope.

'Why is it,' says Richard to Mr Mellendyne, 'that team members on the same side begin to fight among themselves when they near the opposing goal?'

'It is not just the honour of scoring the goal that excites them,' says Moses. 'Each scorer receives two pence for his trouble and free ale for the rest of the day.'

There is something of a lull in the action; the two teams have coalesced into a heaving mass on the north side of the churchyard. Such is the force exerted by each side that the only movement is sideways, first towards the river wall and now the whole mass of men is bearing down on the door of The Fleece. Next door to The Fleece to the north, there is a fine old half-timbered house with a balcony over the street. Richard and John Kettle are leaning out of the window of the upper room, thinking the whole edifice may be brought crashing down if the entangled teams continue their sideways movement, when a thin young man, dressed entirely in a blue and white doublet and leggings, with his face painted in the same two colours and a cap with bells, appears on the next door balcony, leaps onto the sill, throws wide his arms and cries, 'To me! to me!'

The heaving throng pauses for an instant and looks up and around, allowing some quick-thinking denizen of Trinity beneath the scrum to wrench the ball clear and fling it up towards the capering jester. He catches the pigskin in one hand and swings up immediately onto the roof of the house and races off across the tiles, back towards Broad Street. John Kettle makes it onto the back stairs of The Fleece in time to see him disappear over the far rooftops.

'I was wondering if "Jack-Be-Quick" would put in an appearance,' says Moses, mopping his brow, 'and I must say it was very timely today, or the front of my inn may have been stoved in by those fellows. I suggest it's safe to follow the game up the street again, if you want to see anything. Jack will have to come down at some point to cross over, and the St Mary's boys will be waiting for him!'

They reach the square just in time to see Jack-Be-Quick, now on the highest part of the roof of The King's Head, perform a handstand and kick the pigskin further into the air. It spins into the afternoon sun, and those on the ground shade their eyes to mark its fall. When they have rubbed their eyes and look about them, they see a giant arm appear from the melee, and Augustyn lumbering around the corner of The Three Tuns into Broad Street again.

You will remember the rope across the street. Two men are pressed against the wall, in the shadows at the top of Brandy Lane. One of them draws a knife. A head peers around into Bridge Street.

'It's him, he's a-coming!'

Given that they had thought of it all by themselves, it really had all the makings of quite a good plan. Mr

Belwood, whose official puritan position on such sports is one of disapproval, has nevertheless encouraged, and possibly even ordered, Mr Vyner and Mr Costerden to take part in the game of football, and has made it known that any slight misfortune that befalls the party from Norwich would not go amiss, and might well be rewarded. Thus, having witnessed Augustyn's earlier advance up Broad Street, Mr Nicholas and Mr Simon reasoned among themselves that given his size and strength, and the whole afternoon before them, a repeat performance was more than likely, and that a thin piece of rope stretched at jugular height across the street might arrest his progress.

'Allowing us to retrieve the pigskin,' says Nicholas Vyner, 'and with luck he may break his neck and I'll be able to prick him a couple of times with this.'

He runs his finger along the blade of his dagger.

'Not a bad plan at all!' says Humfry, peering out through the windows of The Green Dragon.

'Mr Gildersleeves, if you will join me outside for a few moments, I think you may witness some innocent amusement.'

Augustyn is building up to full speed and looking behind at his failing pursuers when he makes contact with the rope. Such was the force with which he meets it and the depth of Humfry's cut, that it causes only a momentary pause in the giant's headlong rush. At this precise moment, Nicholas and Simon leap out into the street, expecting to find a prone, twitching victim who they can puncture at will.

'Ouch!' says Humfry, with an involuntary wince, as Augustyn runs right through Nicholas Vyner, trampling him into the dusty street.

'Oooooff!' says Mr Gildersleeves. 'T'other won't be presenting to the fair sex for a goodly while, either!'

It is all a matter of gravity. If you leap out from a dark corner, knife at the ready and arms and legs akimbo, and expect to be descending onto your victim who has been brought to the ground, there is no time to adjust your movement or your arrangement of limbs, should you find him still upright and moving forward in a purposeful manner. Thus, the full force of Augustyn's right fist, pumping away on the end of his arm as he runs forward, meets a slightly lesser, but still powerful force as it comes into contact with the groin of Simon Costerden, travelling in the opposite direction. Simon lets out a yell which raises every duck on the nearby river and writhes about in the dirt, crying and moaning and clutching at his doublet. Augustyn stops for a moment and is helping a still groggy Nicholas to his feet when Humfry creeps up beside him, pushes the ball out of his armpit, and races off down Brandy Lane. As he rounds the corner into Nethergate Street, his foot slips on something and he nearly falls. The pigskin flies from his grasp, but only into the arms of two men in yellow and green, who hail him "thanks", and rush off up Bridge Street.

Humfry sits beneath a tree on the corner of the sun-dappled street, getting his breath back. A man appears from the door of the nearby Chequers Inn and approaches him.

'Good day, Master Trip, here is a glass of ale for ye, and good fortune to St Mary's!'

It is Mr Garlicke, the innkeeper.

'Why, Mr Trip, have you hurt yourself? It seems you are bleeding!'

He kneels down and points to Humfry's right boot, which is indeed dark red and dis-coloured.

'Not that I know of,' says Humfry, pulling off his boot. His foot is unscathed but the sole and toe of his boot are covered in dark, slippery blood.

'I stumbled on that corner there,' says Humfry, 'at the end of Brandy Lane. Come with me a moment, Mr Garlicke.'

Brandy Lane runs for most of its length between two high walls, but opens out a little into Bridge Street with a clump of bushes beneath overhanging trees. A thin trickle of blood has seeped out from beneath one of the bushes and formed a pool, into which Humfry had stepped a few moments before. He draws his knife and pushes himself through the bushes.

'Can you see anything, Mr Trip?' calls Mr Garlicke from the lane.

'There is a body here,' says Humfry, 'and much blood. Enough to make the gorge rise.'

'A murder?' cries Mr Garlicke.

'A death, certainly,' says Humfry, 'and not long since, it seems, for his body is still warm. Who or whatever killed him may still be about. You to your inn, Mr Garlicke, and I will inform the reeve and the captain.'

The town reeve is disinclined to halt the football, on account of a mere murder.

'If I try and bring the game to a halt, there may be several other murders,' says the doctor. 'First among them the town reeve and any available feoffees. I will undertake to close off Brandy Lane and the southern end of Bridge Street, so we can proceed without interruption.'

'Humfry, go and fetch Augustyn,' says the captain. 'The game must continue without you both.'

This is easier said than done. It's not difficult to find Augustyn, just follow the screams and look out for the flying bodies, but attracting his attention is quite another matter. If we were there in the flesh, as it were, we might advise Humfry that removing his green and yellow favour might be a good idea, as Augustyn is developing a tendency to fling first and establish identity afterwards. Still, picking through the groaning and the fallen, we eventually locate him near the north wall of St Mary's, now engaged in a mighty struggle against what appears to be the entire female population of the village of Ditchingham, identified by a long yellow banner on which the device "Ditchingham Dames" has been scrawled. You might think this an underhand, low tactic, sending unprincipled women from over the river in against a chivalrous, gentle giant, and you'd be quite right.

Augustyn carefully picks up each female assailant by grasping her around the waist with both hands, and setting her down behind him. The "dames" meanwhile, kick, punch, scratch and assail him with sticks and stones.

Humfry's mother always brought him up to respect the gentler sex, but on this occasion he does it find it necessary to cosh one or two of the larger, more moustachioed ladies, in order to get close enough to Augustyn to attract his attention.

'Gus, Gus, it's me!' yells Humfry, climbing upon the rump of the harpy he has just felled and waving his arms in the giant's face. 'The captain needs you to come right now!'

Augustyn puts down the scratching, spitting spitfire he is holding, picks up Humfry, and places him on his shoulder.

'The ball, Gus!' says Humfry into his ear. 'Get rid of the ball!'

Just beyond the seething mass of dames there is an ancient rock, on which are perched three men in blue and white favours who have been laughing uproariously at Augustyn's travails, while offering him no assistance whatsoever.

Humfry wrenches the ball out from Augustyn's armpit and tosses it to the merry trio.

'Try laughing that off,' says Humfry, as the women turn as one and envelop the three men, whose laughter quickly turns to shrieking.

'I don't think some of those women play quite by the rules,' says Humfry as they pass through the churchyard gate into St Mary's Street.

A small huddle forms at the end of Brandy Lane: the reeve, the captain, Mr Mellendyne, Mr Garlicke, Humfry and Augustyn.

'His head has been nearly torn off,' says Doctor Gordon, 'and has been so chewed as to cloak his identity, at least to me. There are several bites and scratches on his body, and here his ankle is all but severed, as if he was dragged under here by whatever slew him. I cannot see any stab wounds from dagger or sword. From his ragged clothes I would say he was a poor man, although they were much disturbed by the attacker.'

Neither Mr Garlicke nor Mr Mellendyne, who as publicans make it their business to know as much as they can about as many of the town's population as they can manage, will hazard even a guess as to who this poor unfortunate might be, and the captain is on the point of instructing Augustyn to wrap the body in a sheet and convey it to the charnel house, when the giant pauses in his labours, takes Humfry by the shoulder and points at the corpse.

'Yes, I've seen all I want to see, Gus – it's 'orrible, I don't need to see – what, what about his 'and? Blimey, you're right, it's old "Wassha-knee-no"! Sorry, Captain, he was a drunk we met in The Falcon the other night. I noticed his left 'and didn't 'ave no thumb nor forefinger, and didn't 'ave time to ask him why before Gus here prised him off me.'

'Is this the man you told me had claimed to have seen the black dog?' says Richard.

'Yes, he's the one,' says Humfry, 'said he knew all about it, and what did we know? Well, the poor sod never saw nothin' this time!'

'I think we have our man, now, Captain,' Moses says, 'and Mr Garlicke will bear with me, these are the remains of Tranter Bowtell, formerly a respected citizen in this town, and a seller of pots and pans and other ironmongery in a shop once adjacent to The Fleece. He fell into ruin some years ago and has not been seen in Bongay for some months.'

Captain Brightwell stands in the churchyard, gazing up at the tower of St Mary's, stark and bright beneath a full moon. It's been quite a day, one way or another. The football continues until seven o'clock, when at 3–3, the survivors of the opposing teams agree that they are too drunk, exhausted or appallingly injured to continue. Or the latter two, as they have immediately retired to the various alehouses to relive every moment of the afternoon in minute detail, fuelled by several more tankards of ale. The captain is pleased with the result, and the participation of Humfry and Augustyn, as it might have helped in gaining the confidence of the townsfolk, without alienating either parish. There had, of course, been a violent and grisly murder today, but if you wish to investigate such an event and dispose of the corpse quietly without unduly alarming the populace, then you could not stick a pin in a calendar and find a better date than the day of the annual parish football match. It might be necessary to give John Kettle relief from his duties as a scribe for tomorrow morning, and send him to The Falcon and to the town reeve to find out more about the unfortunate Mr Bowtell. Richard is about to sit down upon a mound in the churchyard, the better to enjoy the moonlight, when he discovers it is snoring, and is in fact, a heap of recumbent footballers, worn out by their exertions and about two gallons of ale apiece. There is also Mr Denny and his hole-in-the-wall to consider; and he has yet to ascend the bell tower to see the place where (some had it) the bodies of Fuller and

Walker had been found. And to think how Humfry had complained of how dull this expedition was likely to be! And there was that look Miss Kindred had given him, near this very spot, out from under her eyebrows, with the scent of new-baked bread wafting from her basket as she passed by him.

Miss Kindred? What had she to do with anything? That had been two days ago. Where had she appeared from in his thoughts?

'Er – Captain, begging your pardon, Mr Mellendyne wishes to know would you join him in a glass before closing, sir?'

SEVEN

'You are sure, sir,' says John Kettle, concern creasing his forehead, 'that you will be able to act as scribe in my absence?'

'It will, of course, take a little longer,' says Richard, 'but I anticipate no difficulty, and it will only be for an hour or so!'

Richard has met all manner of men in the army but is relatively inexperienced in the ways of women, and especially in the ways of women like Mrs Jekell, who is his first interviewee of the morning. Mrs Jekell is one of those women who views each day as a trial to be got through, and every event in each day as a necessary hindrance. She refuses to make any distinction in each day between, say, the sun shining or the rain falling. Mrs Jekell was at the service on August 4th, and yes, she supposed there had been some sort of storm, and that it had been rather dark for an August morning (although back in '46, when she'd been but a girl that had been black as night one day at noon in July, so she remembered). Captain Brightwell, scribbling furiously, begins to appreciate the efficacy of being able to ask questions without having himself to record the answers. Yes, she had heard the thunder and seen the flashes of lightning, and no, she had not made anything of that. A particular storm, of which she had thought nothing, until her husband (who was away at the coast and could not come today) had read her Mr Fleming's little book, and of course there must have been a dog, otherwise how would those poor men have come to such an end? And no, she could not describe the creature, but a dog was a dog, and people had said that it was very big and black, so that was likely to be a big black dog? Was that all, as today is market day, and what fish there were would be gone if she did not make shift!

The captain nods and half-rises as she leaves; his wrist is aching mightily and he has only got as far as copying the part about Mr Fleming's book and the dog, when there comes a soft knock on the door to the stairs, which is pushed gently ajar.

'Excuse us, sir, we were sent up by my uncle – by Mr Mellendyne. Miss Poope and Miss Kindred?'

The captain nods his head in silence for a full twenty seconds before realising he has his mouth open and must appear to the young women as if he has lost his wits.

'Come in,' he gargles, 'please sit down.'

Richard sits behind his desk, all speech flown. He looks at the pert Miss Poope, and into the deep, brown eyes of Miss Kindred. A pregnant pause ensues. So very long a pregnant pause that it might have been born, coddled, weaned and taken its first faltering steps before Captain Brightwell could find it in himself to give utterance.

Miss Poope is the first to break the silence.

'Your—' she says.

'My scribe, yes!' says the captain. 'John Kettle! He's not here.'

He points at John's empty chair.

'He's somewhere else, doing – something else – for me, which is why he's not here.'

The captain knows he must sound like a great fool, and wants to appear calm and urbane, and in control, but every time he catches Miss Kindred's eye his mind shuts down and he begins to spout drivel.

'You are very kind to see us together,' says Miss Poope, carefully, 'as we are not kin, but are merely friends who were at the service at the same time.'

The captain barely hears a word beyond "together"; the thought that he might have been alone in this room with Miss Cicely Kindred with those eyes and only a table between them, brings on another bout of babbling.

'So today I have to make my own notes,' he says, holding up his quill, as if proof were needed, 'and although well practised in letters, I am not as used as John Kettle is to the speed at which people will talk, although there are many in this town that do dwell on their words – John says, and—'

'Captain!' says Anna. 'Do not concern yourself, we are not silly girls, and do not run on in that way.'

'Whatever you ask,' says Cicely, 'we will endeavour to answer.'

A mighty struggle is going on within the captain. The cool level-headed, military side of his mind has accepted this sensible, rational, quietly spoken statement, and is preparing to frame an equally intelligent question in response. The other side of his mind, which has only made itself fully known in the last few minutes; thinks that, "whatever you ask, we will endeavour to answer", is just about the most lascivious thing that has ever been said by anyone to anybody, ever.

Let us leave them for a while; this is, after all, an adventure rather than a romance. You may stay if you wish, but on this occasion neither Anna nor Cicely will tell him anything he has not heard already from others, and that is an awful scrawl he is making on John Kettle's parchment, and nothing much else will happen for half an hour or so, except a baker's boy passing beneath their open window, and the smell of freshly baked bread un-manning the captain all over again so that he tips over the inkwell, and knocks a deal of paper on to the floor, which Cicely and Anna help him to retrieve. Anna thinks the captain is quite off his head but has begun to rather like him. Cicely thinks – well, never mind what Cicely thinks for now, let us go and find Master Kettle.

His commission is to visit the town reeve and The Falcon Inn to discover more of the origins and character of the unfortunate Tranter Bowtell. In his practical way,

John decides to favour the town reeve with his first call, working on the assumption that the good doctor will be up early working on his prescriptions, before sallying forth later in the day to tend to the sick and the palsied of Bongay. The denizens of The Falcon Inn, who on the whole tend to regard the midday sun as the approach of daybreak, will be therefore worthy of a later visit. Also, John intends to descend upon The Falcon accompanied by Augustyn and Humfry, in case any of the good citizens there take exception to his questioning.

Doctor Gordon lives in a fine house under the castle wall on the road to Earsham. John has to walk through a narrow tunnel from the street, and finds himself in a small, but well-tended garden. The door of the house is open, and John calls, "Hallo!" to raise anybody who is about.

Doctor Gordon appears from behind a large bay tree, a small knife in one hand, and a wooden bowl in the other.

'Ah yes!' he says quite calmly, as if he has been expecting a visit. 'You are Mr Kettle, the captain's…? Excuse this, I am collecting some herbs for my – er – potations? Would you mind holding the…?'

He hands John the bowl, and cuts some sprigs of bay, rosemary and thyme, and two large sage leaves.

'I believe I would come here and rub the leaves of a morning, even if they were not at all efficacious,' sighs the doctor. 'Lady Sherborne, when she was the prioress, kept a herb garden that was renowned throughout this part of the country. All, sadly, long…'

John Kettle has to stop himself adding "gone" to this last sentiment.

'You wish to discover anything of interest in Mr Bowtell?' says Doctor Gordon. 'Sadly there is not much to tell. He was a solid citizen, and an honest tradesman for many years; but then fell into some speculation that resulted in his… he then left the town, and was not heard of until several months ago when he began appearing in The Falcon, and making a vast nuisance of himself. He was living in a hut by the river, but how he kept body and soul together, I know not!'

'Do you know how he met his death?' says John.

'With extreme vio-lence,' says the doctor, 'but not, by any human hand, at least, not directly. He was severely mauled by a large creature, as yet unknown, with very sharp teeth and claws.'

'Do you know of any such creature?' says John.

'Not that is not of fancy and legend,' says the doctor, 'not known in this quiet land.'

'This man mentioned to my companions – admittedly while in his cups – that he had seen the "Black Dog" that everyone has been speaking of lately. Could these wounds have been caused by such a dog?'

'By no ordi-nary dog, certainly,' says Doctor Gordon, 'but I am led to believe the beast, whatever it was, was under some other command.'

'Forgive me,' says John, 'I cannot follow your—'

'Mr Bowtell was not prey to this animal,' says the doctor. 'He was grievously wounded, but no part of him was…'

'Eaten?' says John.

'Devoured!' says the doctor, raising his eyebrows and staring wide-eyed at John. 'I believe that Tranter Bowtell was killed quite deliberately.'

He puts together his hands in an attitude of prayer.

'May God have mercy on his... Some will be saying in the town that the shade of Hugh Bigod has returned. Bigod built the castle, you understand, in the days of King Stephen. There is a tale here that he kept a foul creature in his dungeon that he would release each New Year's Day, and which would not return until it had savaged and slain one of the townsfolk?'

'I have heard that story,' says John.

'It is what many believe,' says the doctor.

'Of course,' he goes on, 'Bowtell is not the first man of iron-mongery in this place to meet with misfortune, there was Cowper, who had a similar shop on the Earsham Road for many... He came to me with the gout, and dropsy and a palsy brought on by too much wine, and do you know what?'

The doctor raises his eyebrows almost to his hairline and beams quizzically at John Kettle.

'I cured him! With the aid of his family we stole away and hid all the strong drink in the house, forbade him the door of the vintners, cut his meals to three a day, and made him walk everywhere, and especially up and down Bridge Street four times a day!'

'Well done!' says John Kettle. 'But you said he met with misfortune. How so? Where is he now?'

'Dead!' exclaims the doctor. 'Drownded in the river! Part of his new way of living was to paddle in a skiff on the river twice a day. He caught his oar in a sunken bush, went over the side and sank beneath the water, never to rise hence!'

The doctor gives another of his wide-eyed, wan little smiles.

'Of course, I did not say so to Mrs Cowper, she being consumed with grief, but it struck me as a great irony! If Mr Cowper had been of his former girth, he would most likely have bobbed to the surface like an apple, and been pulled to the shore and safety. As it was, he being mostly now bone and little flesh, he sank like a stone!

'But of course,' he goes on, 'if he had been still been stout, he would not have been in the boat in the first... Which only proves that there is no potion yet brewed which can still the hand of fate. Now I beg you, I must be about my patients still not savaged by beasts or overcome by the river, so please excuse me. You may go out as you came in!'

At the conclusion of this uplifting little homily he shakes John warmly by the hand and disappears into his house.

Half an hour later John Kettle is striding down Bridge Street, with Humfry and Augustyn in tow.

'The Falcon,' says John. 'What manner of alehouse is it?'

Humfry looks at Augustyn, who shrugs his massive shoulders.

'It's, er, well – it's not like The Fleece,' says Humfry.

'How so?' says John Kettle.

'It is an alehouse, like The Fleece, but it is not an inn, or at least not much like an inn, there are no rooms like ours – but people do sleep there, but usually on the floor, overcome in their cups.'

On entering the taproom John finds that nearly all the clientele are up and moving, and are sitting around various tables, blinking in the late morning sun that is trying in vain to flood in through the grimy windows.

John accosts an ill-favoured pot-boy and asks to see the innkeeper.

'Mr Strine is above, and does not see no one 'til he pleases,' mutters the pot-boy.

'That is a terrible squint you have on you, young 'un,' says Humfry, 'so I'll be of good charity and assume you cannot look a gentleman like Master Kettle here straight in the eye and answer him when he asks you a civil question? Tell Mr Strine above that Mr John Kettle is here on the authority of Captain Brightwell, and see if that pleases him; and if it don't, that Mr Flowerdew here will shortly be up to fetch him.'

The pot-boy scuttles off up a dark stairwell. At the mention of "Mr Flowerdew", there are a number of hoots and guffaws from the assembled company.

'God love us, little man!' calls out one worthy. 'That's a lovely soft name you have! Were you born in a cowslip?'

'Or did you fall out of a daffydilly?' says another.

Humfry holds up a hand.

'Cease, good men! You are mistooken. My name is Humfry Trip – this fellow here is Mr Augustyn Flowerdew!'

There is a great collective sigh from the members of the taproom, something like the air being expelled slowly from a giant pig's bladder.

'I'm sure we meant no harm,' says the first worthy.

'No,' says a second, ''tis a fine and manly name, such as anyone – seven feet tall – would be proud to own.'

'Perhaps they would think "John Kettle" a fine name, if I were seven feet tall?' mutters John under his breath.

'Perhaps,' says Humfry. 'Hearken! There is some commotion from on high!'

It is the pot-boy, descending the stairs at a run and a crouch, with several small objects, books and bric-a-brac bouncing off his person as he comes, and assailed by oaths and imprecations from above.

'Git down those bliddy stairs, yew useless artickle! Flowerdew, indeed! Brightwell, by his mother, no better than she ever was! Kettle, black as night, and dancing on the hob as he should be! What manner of a name is that, pray!'

'I know not, and care less,' cries the pot-boy, rubbing his head and fleeing to the cellar.

Here is Mr Strine, at the foot of the stairs; let us pause and drink him in for a moment. Have you ever seen anything so pink and glowing, and yet as like an egg on legs as he, perfectly rotund, and bald and shiny?

'I would fear for his safety if he sat on a wall!' murmurs Humfry.

Mr Strine was not present on the occasion of their last visit, so spends a few moments gazing up at Augustyn, and adjusting his language and demeanour accordingly.

'God save you, Master Kettle, and yourn – er, companions! Will you take a glass of ale?'

'Presently,' says John Kettle, 'I'm given to understand that Tranter Bowtell used to frequent this inn?'

'Him that was savaged during the football?'

Mr Strine rubs one of his many chins and tries to look thoughtful.

'The same,' says John.

'Yes!' says Mr Strine. 'It is true to say that he called in on more than one occasion, but that is no crime or felony – this is, after all, an alehouse!'

'My companions were accosted by Mr Bowtell on their last visit, when he claimed to have seen something of the "Black Dog". Did he ever speak of this creature to you?'

Mr Strine shrugs the lower part of his neck, where shoulders are on other men.

'I don't recall – he was always crazed about something or other, and everyone's been talking of "seeing the dog" lately, ever since it come to St Mary's!'

'But he said more!' says Humfry. 'Saving your presence, Master Kettle – he said he had seen the dog, and knew who had sent it?'

'In his dreams, mayhap!' scoffs Mr Strine. 'Or his nightmares. His wits had deserted him these many years, I do not think you can take account of anything he said.'

''Tis quite heavy wit for the time of day,' says Humfry, as they walked back up Bridge Street, 'but I don't think it wise to take account of anything much of what Mr Strine has said, neither!'

'Either,' murmurs John Kettle.

On their return to The Fleece, Captain Brightwell is nowhere to be found.

'He was here not ten minutes ago,' says Mr Mellendyne. 'He was going for a walk to clear his mind – he did look a little distracted. He said to have your dinner directly, Mr Kettle, and that he would inspect the tower of St Mary's at two o'clock?'

Nothing remarkable had been said during the interview between Richard and Anna Poope and Cicely Kindred; but Richard feels profoundly unsettled by the experience. He strides out across the common on a path to the north of the town, which is bounded by the bend in the river. The common is mostly pasture land, with just a few trees on the river bank and a solitary oak about half a league hence. Though it is not long past noon, it has become a dull, louring day, with thick, grey cloud blowing in from the sea. Richard pulls his hat down and leans into the wind.

Miss Cicely Kindred. What a soft rounded name is "Cicely"! Captain Brightwell has a mother and a sister, but knows little else of the ways of women, having never been one for the stews and easy-houses of city or campaign. Thus, he finds himself quite overtaken by Miss Kindred. He is at a loss to know why, when he asks pretty, lively, attractive Miss Anna Poope what she saw of the Black Dog, her answer of "nothing, sir", elicits a tick in the margin and nought else; yet when the same question is stammered out to Cicely, her answer of "I cannot be sure, sir" makes him snap the nib of his quill and upset the inkpot again. (John Kettle, on seeing the mayhem done to his desk and papers, fears there must have been a fight.)

Richard stops on the path. "I cannot be sure, sir." While taking a stray tendril of dark hair and tucking it behind her ear, and freeing the hem of her dress from her heel. It was the sort of thing women did all the time. But never with such grace. The sky is growing darker by the minute, and the wind blows stronger. Richard is thirty yards short of the tree. Far in the distance to his left, across the white fields, he espies a dark shape. It is moving at great speed and is running in a straight line in the direction of the town to his right. Richard shades his eyes and peers into the gloom. He has reached the tree and stands beneath its branches, as a light rain begins to fall. As it draws near, Richard thinks it about the size and shape of a young heifer, but loping along very swiftly, with easy strides. It will cross his path some hundred yards beyond the tree. Richard is still not sure what manner of creature it is, so steps out from the shade of the tree to get a better view. The animal stops on the path, as if catching the sudden movement, raises its head, and sniffs the air. Richard's body temperature has been altering somewhat already this day, every time he thinks of Miss Kindred's clear brown eyes, but now his veins turn to ice. It is far too big to be a dog, but then heifers do not snarl and slaver, and paw the ground. The beast pads slowly towards the tree, snuffling back and forth along the path. It stops again, raises its head and sniffs the air once more.

Richard has not done any tree climbing since he was a boy, and the lower branches are nearly six feet off the ground, but it is amazing how agile craven fear can make a man, and by the time the beast reaches the tree he is thirty feet up among the branches. As it prowls around the base of the trunk, and leaps up at him, Richard tries to remember whether any of the extensive literature he's read about phantom dogs in the last few weeks said anything about their ability to climb trees. After a few minutes, it tires of this sport, lies down at the base of the trunk, and appears to fall into a doze.

Fearing a trap, Richard settles himself securely in a fork of the tree, and prepares to wait. After a few minutes, and sheltered from the strong wind by the leaves and branches, he too dozes off.

He is awakened by a low moaning. It is not the wind, which has wafted away, and it is not a sound he has ever heard any dog make. At the foot of the tree there is a figure in dark clothes with a black scarf over its head. The dog is nowhere to be seen. Richard's foot slips a little and the figure raises its head. He catches a glimpse of a woman's face. It is not an ill-favoured nor beautiful face, but stern and benign, and full of sorrow. There are shouts of "Holloa" from the path leading to the town. The dark shape is gone in an instant, melting into the rank grass.

EIGHT

The weather is changeable in these parts and at this season, so let us go in search of the sun, and move westwards of the lowering skies above Bongay, about a mile or so, and sit atop a grassy bank by the roadside from Bury St Edmunds. Enjoy the big blue sky, and the elevated cloud formations that pass for mountains among these people of the east. The road is quiet today, just one wagon in half an hour, which turns off on the lane to Alburgh. Just as you begin to wonder why we have been brought to this pleasant but undeniably quiet spot, a figure appears out of the west.

A small un-prepossessing man, in a long black coat, riding on a rather wheezy and wizened pony appears over the rise. We cannot make out much of his features, as he wears a wide-brimmed felt hat, but we can hear him murmuring as he passes, what appear to be prayers and incantations. It's just as well we can't hear them, because he is praying that God will visiteth his wrath on the people of Harleston, who, tiring lately of his rants and exhortations, threatened to duck him in the river if he did not cease the same. He adds a further prayer for the eternal damnation of the people of Diss who, being less sanguine than their northern neighbours, had tipped our devout traveller into their mere two days since, and only fished him out on his promise to depart immediately. There is an air of dampness and darkness about pony and rider, even in this bright sunshine, and they appear to be steaming slightly.

Upon rounding a slight bend in the road, they espy a tall church tower lying to the south. The rider dismounts, removes a small stool from his pack, kneels upon it by the roadside and begins to loudly proclaim the manifold sins and wickedness of the people of Bongay, and that God bring down his judgement upon them.

At which point, two local worthies appear from behind a hayrick in an adjacent field and inform our man of God that the tower to which he is gesticulating is that of Redenhall Church, and that he is disturbing their midday repose, and thank him for his concern and his prayers, but he had better be on his way, and that Bongay lies a good six leagues hence.

In spite of their words, the two men don't look very thankful, and one of them is grasping a pitchfork, and being only too aware that there is a river in the vicinity, our pilgrim hastily packs up his stool, and urges his pony eastwards.

This then, is our first encounter with the Reverend Abram Fleming, without whom, indeed, we would have no story to tell. We will leave him now, as there will be more than enough of him later. He is still some miles short of Bongay, and will take an age to reach it, as he has a habit of stopping every few hundred yards or so, pulling out a leather-covered notebook, and writing down observations on the weather, landscape, flora and fauna.

'Humfry! Do not be alarmed, I am almost down! Did you see anything on the path these last few minutes?'

'Only Gus's old pig, sir, just now, hunting truffles over by the North Gate.'

Richard drops lightly to the ground and dusts some twigs from his breeches.

'Augustyn's pig?' says Richard.

'Just another animal about the town he has befriended,' says Humfry. 'A regular little St Francis, our Gus is.'

'You saw no dog of any sort, or a woman on the path?'

'Er – no sir?' says Humfry, eying the captain with some concern. 'We – er, heard from Mr Mellendyne that you appeared somewhat distracted, and as the day was advancing beyond noon came to look for you?'

'Do not concern yourself, I needed some distraction, certainly, but just those of exercise and fresh air. Now, I must be away to the church,' says Richard. 'Humfry, you are to take Augustyn and find Ellen Peele and the other women who laid out Adam Walker and John Fuller, and bring them to the upper room at half past two o'clock. You may assure them of their safety and of our goodwill.'

'Why is it,' says John Kettle, sitting in the porch of St Mary's, 'that the people of this district say: "We are now going", instead of the common usage, "We are going now"?'

'Perhaps people in other parts of the kingdom are not as animated as our folk?' says Thomas Rune. John casts his mind back over some of the "animated folk" he has encountered in the last two days. Miss Annable Jolly and her companions were certainly animated, and Mr Belwood also, but in a darker way.

'Mmmm, perhaps,' he murmurs.

'If you are here on market day,' says Cornelius, 'when folk come in from the South Elmhams and the Ilketshalls, you will soon be made aware that their speech can vary over quite short distances, and that some cannot be made out at all. Ah, here is your captain, all in a rush!'

'God save you!' says Richard. 'And forgive me my tardiness.'

'It is not ten minutes since the hour struck,' says Thomas, 'and we were pleasantly engaged with Master Kettle here, on comparing local customs of speech.'

'I would very much like to see the belfry and the bell chamber,' says Richard, 'and be shown where Masters Fuller and Walker met their deaths?'

They ascend a steep wooden ladder in the base of the tower, which leads them to the ringing chamber. The room is charred and burnt, the roof timbers are split, three of the ropes hang broken, and there is a general air of desolation.

'This is where Adam and John should have been,' says Cornelius, 'if they were ringing before the service. And if this room was struck by a lightning bolt, as seems all too probable, then they would certainly have been much injured, or killed.'

'But surely there is some witness?' says Richard. 'Someone who first came upon them?'

'The clerk says they were killed in the belfry, but others speak of their bodies being discovered in the body of the church,' says Thomas.

'And after Fleming's tract appeared, there are many who will now swear they were in the congregation throughout the service,' says Cornelius.

'Well,' says John Kettle, 'someone is mistaken – they could not have been seen to be slain in two places at once!'

They pass down the ladder and into the church.

'There was such noise and darkness and confusion that morning that it is difficult to piece together any coherent sequence of events,' says Cornelius.

'If we cannot establish where they died, perhaps we should look more closely into exactly how they died,' says John Kettle.

'God save you once more, gentlemen,' says Richard, shaking hands with the Rune brothers. 'We are to meet with Ellen Peele at half past the hour.'

Ellen Peele has seen death in all its forms, and has, as she proudly boasts to Captain Brightwell, "Laid out every corpse in Bongay these past twenty year," except those who had died of plague of course, as she had no wish to be one of their number quite yet.

Richard asks why she has come alone, and Ellen explains that the other two women who assist her, while good dames, are as poor in mind as they are in body, and cannot make a sentence between them. As Ellen herself has a mad left eye, about three teeth, and shouts all her speech, Richard is disposed to be relieved rather than upset at their absence.

'Now what do I know?' says Ellen.

'I understand you and the other good women laid out the bodies of Masters Fuller and Walker, after the service on the 4th August last?' says Richard.

'I do know that!' says Ellen. 'God have mercy on their poor dear souls, but was not straight after, you understand – there were all the people to be got out and the poor griped boy. We were not called in until the afternoon.'

'Who asked for you?' says Richard.

'Mr Belwood, at least it was his man, Nicholas Vyner, who come a-knocking an' a hollering at my door. Said we was to lay out the bodies for burial so they could be disposed of in the morning.'

'Is that in the ordinary way of things?' says John Kettle.

'Oh yes, sir,' says Ellen, 'specially in this hot season – and unless the family have to come from afar, which was not the case in these cases.'

'Did you or your women notice anything untoward about the bodies when laying them out?' says Richard.

'I've seen men struck by thunderbolts, before, sir,' says Ellen, 'an' they was always blackened and burnt. These two were somewhat hotly singed, but had many other wounds when we had sight of them.'

'So, there were signs of burning on their bodies?' says Richard.

'Oh, yes sir,' says Ellen Peele, 'but they had many wounds and tears as if mauled by some wild beast, deep cuts in their arms and bodies, and Fuller had been gouged about his head, and yet there was a strangeness which both I and Margery noticed.'

'How so?' says Richard.

'Both their necks were purple and swollen,' says Ellen, her swivelling left eye still for a moment, 'like men who have been hanged.'

'As you say, you have seen the dead in many guises,' says Richard. 'Can you say with any certainty how these two men died?'

'No, sir,' says Ellen, 'we are no wiser than the wise who have charge in the town, they could have been killed by the thunderbolt, by the dog that some speak of – or by some other means…'

'Thank you, and here is something for your trouble,' says Richard.

'I am sure you are most kind and generous,' says Ellen, bowing to the captain while rolling her eye at John Kettle. 'I'll wish you gentlemen good day.'

'Well!' says John, rising and opening the window onto the street. 'I'm not sure that leaves us any wiser than the wise, either. It seems that Mr Fuller and Mr Walker had a most unfortunate morning on August 4th! They became accidentally entangled in their bell ropes, causing them to hang themselves, then, while struggling to be free, the tower was struck by a lightning bolt, which roasted them alive, and then, if others are to be believed, they were savaged by a spectral hound, which finally made an end of them! All rather unlucky, I would say, and unlikely, as well!'

'It may not be quite so,' says Richard. 'I want you to take these letters to the town reeve and to the vicar of St Mary's, informing them that Adam Fuller and John Walker are to be exhumed forthwith. It is to be done secretly, this night, and must remain between us.'

The captain has not lived in a small town since childhood, so has forgotten – if he ever learnt – that "from whom no secrets are hidden", applies not only to God; but in a place like Bongay, to just about everyone else in the street.

Just one hour later Richard and John Kettle are attended by a grim delegation of feoffees. They look more than vaguely familiar.

'Now, I am not good with names,' says Richard. 'Messrs Dorlett, Mountell, Grime and Towtinge, if I recall? But I do not know these other two gentlemen?'

One is tall and angular, with dark, lank hair, the other is small and bald and tending to roundness, like a distant cousin of Mr Strine, but better dressed.

'Mr Slapshot!' announces the tall one, with an extravagant bow. 'And this is Mr Grope, we are attorneys-at-law; representing Mr Thomas Belwood.'

'Who, I notice,' says Richard, 'is not with us, again.'

'There are sufficient of us here, I think, to represent his interest!' says Mr Towtinge. 'And indeed our own!'

'And what is your interest?' says Richard.

'Damn, sir!' says Mr Towtinge, growing red-faced and belligerent. 'You who bring riot and murder among us, now seek to dig up—'

'Perhaps, if I may,' says Mr Slapshot, 'cool words rather than hot ones, good sirs? Mr Belwood and these feoffees understand it is your intention to exhume those poor unfortunates slain by the Black Dog in August 4th last. And that such an action will bring great distress to their kinsfolk and spread alarm among the town. As well as being a gross violation to their persons, and a sin before God!'

'Amen!' intoned the feoffees, as one.

'Mr Belwood's intelligence obviously far exceeds my own,' says Richard, 'since the order was given but an hour ago, and then for the eyes only of the town reeve and the vicar of St Mary's!'

'So, you do not deny that this is your intention?' says Mr Slapshot. 'You mean to sully these poor men's souls?'

'I mean to exhume them so I may be satisfied as to how they met their deaths,' says Richard. 'They are dead, and their souls have long since passed to another place, so no one will be sullied, and their remains will be treated with all the respect due to them.'

'I think that Mr Belwood may feel that such a course will be actionable,' says Mr Grope.

'In which case he may apply to the Bishop of Norwich,' says Richard, 'on whose authority I act. Now, I am almost as busy a man as your master, so I bid you all good day!'

They pass down the stairs with many black looks and dark mutterings, and stand for many minutes in a close huddle by the door of The Fleece.

John Kettle observes them from the window of the upper room.

'They seem somewhat concerned,' says John. 'There are raised voices and gesticulations in the direction of St Mary's tower. I think your chances of becoming an honorary feoffee are as slim as Miss Annable Jolly's waist!'

'Ah, you see what can be revealed in an unguarded moment!' says Richard. 'Now I know of what you are daydreaming when some biddy is sat here bemoaning the price of turnips at last Thursday's market.'

John Kettle could have replied that the slenderness of Miss Jolly's waist had not yet driven him to such distraction as wandering on the common pursued by pigs and phantasms, but has not sufficient time nor wit to put it into words.

Mr Moses Mellendyne is among them, mopping his brow and puffing from a precipitate ascent of the stairs.

'S'cuse me, Cap'n, and Mr Kettle, I have just now been informed that a Reverend Fleming has been seen in the town and is attending on Mr Belwood at his residence.'

'Send Humfry Trip to Mr Belwood with my compliments,' says Richard, 'with a request that the Reverend Fleming attend upon us here at his earliest convenience.'

Mr Denny is sitting in the vastness of St Mary's church, gazing at a hole in the wall. He is alone, as his men have gone straight from their dinner to repair a collapsed roof in Bridge Street. Mr Denny hopes that Mr Belwood or his cronies do not pass by them, or he will be here haranguing about his window. Mr Denny is a man of business, and works where he can, but he is quite sure in his mind that upon completion of this window (which to his mind adds nothing at all to the lustre of the building), he will not undertake work for Mr Belwood again. Edmond is raised from his reverie by the sound of men's voices, and of furniture being knocked about. He rises, listens carefully and walks soft-footed and swiftly to the door to the church tower. From the other side of the door there emanate curses and imprecations, and sounds of a struggle. Edmond is sure all of his men are working at Bridge Street and has seen no one pass in or out during the last hour. It does not sound as if whoever is behind the door is about their lawful business. Edmond Denny is a brave and righteous man. He arms himself with a short, stout piece of wood, and raps on the door.

'Halloa! You there! What is that commotion? Show yourselves!'

The door is pulled violently open. Edmond steps back and raises his cudgel.

NINE

'Am I to understand,' says Abram Fleming, 'that after what has occurred, the citizens of this town are still sunk so low in sin and depravity that they indulge in a game of football, no doubt accompanied by much drunken ness and licentiousness, and riotous behaviour? Would they not be better employed upon their knees, praying to Almighty God not to visit further ruin and desolation upon them for their manifold sins and wickedness? Are there no upright and godly men in this sink of iniquity?'

'They – we are but few – I grant you,' says Thomas Belwood. 'But we work—'

'And pray!' snaps Fleming.

'And pray, of course, towards that day when they will seek forgiveness and cast themselves on His mercy.'

'On His judgement!' says the incandescent clergyman. 'They must make account for all their sodomitical sinnes and be punished accordingly, before they can begin to think of mercy!'

They are sitting in Mr Belwood's parlour. Mr Fleming is sipping a glass of wine, to restore him after the travails of his journey. Mr Fleming abhors strong drink as a rule, and preaches against the taking of it at every opportunity, but to spread God's word he needs bodily strength.

'I take no pleasure in this wine,' he reminds Mr Belwood, taking a prodigious gulp, 'except of course in your hospitality in providing it! I take it purely to restore my tissues.'

'As you have had, by your account, such a testing journey,' says Mr Belwood, raising the decanter, 'perhaps you are in need of further restoration?'

'You are more than kind,' says Mr Fleming, proffering his glass.

In truth, Mr Belwood has been a little taken aback by the Reverend Fleming coming upon him in this way. Their last meeting was in London, where the clergyman, while inclined to ranting, had at least appeared soberly dressed and of respectable mien. This rather mad looking and wild-eyed shabbily dressed prophet is far too Old Testament for Mr Belwood's taste, and he suspects that if this present apparition is presented to the townspeople as the author and origin of the Black Dog phenomena, a certain amount of derision might ensue.

'I understand you are keen to inspect the town, and especially the scene of the visitation,' says Mr Belwood, 'but I must prevail upon you to rest after your ordeal, and er, perhaps something can be done for your attire? Have some more wine!'

Mr Belwood's servant is with us, and announces that Master Humfry Trip is without, with a missive from Captain Brightwell, which is to be delivered in person and by hand.

'Save ye, Mr B!' says Humfry, upon his entrance. 'To spare you the trouble of reading, the cap'n would like some time with Mr Fleming at his earliest convenience! Oh, is this the reverend gentleman here, sir? Good day, come a long way today – you look as if it were so?'

'From Harleston, though why a servant should think he can address me so!' says Mr Fleming. 'Come, Belwood, what "captain" is this fellow speaking of, and what truck must I have with him?'

It is not often that Humfry can tower over a fellow man, but he draws himself up to his full height and glares down upon the miniscule Fleming.

'Captain, Richard Brightwell, to you – sir!' says Humfry. 'Here by the authority of His Lord the Bishop of Norwich, and commissioned to hear all who have claimed to have seen anything supernatural or untoward on the 4th August, last, about which you seem to have so much knowledge.'

'Mr Fleming is much discommoded by his journey,' says Mr Belwood, 'inform the captain we will see him on the morrow! Now go, begone!'

Mr Edmond Denny is lying on the floor of St Mary's, staring at the ceiling. He is not thinking about anything, for he is in fact, almost dead. Three of his men, having repaired the roof in Bridge Street, have just discovered his body by the tower door. He is stretched on his back with his arms in the air. His throat is much torn, and there is a trail of gore and bloody tracks leading to the open door of the porch. Augustyn, who visits the church about this time every day, meets two of Denny's men at the door as they rush out to raise the alarm. They are white-faced and crying and mewing, and flap their arms at Augustyn, and point at the remains of their good master.

Augustyn picks up the broken body with infinite care, and places it on a bench at the back of the church. He tears down one of the sheets around Mr Belwood's window and covers Edmond Denny from the world's glare. He is found there by Richard and Doctor Gordon some minutes later.

'Why would anyone, or thing, want to attack Mr Edmond Denny?' says Richard.

'Even a good man may have enemies,' says Doctor Gordon, lifting the sheet and examining Edmond's wounds. 'And sometimes even the act of doing good will make them so.'

'I only met him twice,' says the captain, 'but I found him an honest, straightforward sort of man, not afraid to speak his mind.'

'He was just so,' says the doctor. 'Perhaps a *little* more fearfulness and he might still be among the living. His throat has been torn horribly, and the back of his skull is split, as if he was hit to the ground, and his chest is much bruised. It may be he was attacked from the front, forced down and eviscerated where he lay. I cannot say at what point life left his body, or indeed, God save us, if it has! Quick, Master Flowerdew, bring him to my house, I felt a faint breath upon my hand this moment! Away, while he may live!'

'I wish we could have discovered him before his men,' sighs Richard. 'This attack may consume the town with fear and wild rumour.'

Fear and wild rumour have indeed, wasted not a moment. A large number of people have gathered in the square, where there is talk of the Black Dog returning to the church tower, and slaying the master mason, and three of his men, and that Edmond Denny has died for being a blasphemer, and that his wife is a witch and his children sprites, and that the town needs to be cleansed of evil spirits.

'No!' cries John Kettle, addressing those who will listen from the porch of The King's Head. 'It was three of his men who brought the news of the attack on the master mason, who are alive and under safekeeping in The Fleece Inn, and Mr Denny's wife and children are being comforted there also, under the protection of Mr Flowerdew.'

This last piece of information calms everybody down a bit, those, mostly denizens of The Falcon, who a few moments ago were all for bringing out "the witch" and branding her and her little demons, suddenly recall that Mr Flowerdew is about eight feet tall, and begin to reconsider. Perhaps Mr Denny was just in the wrong place at the wrong time; and that his wife and children are as pleasant and unremarkable as they have always appeared to be before this afternoon.

That is, until a small dark, bedraggled figure appears upon a box amidst the heaving throng.

'By the grace of Almighty God, I have come to you in this time of great calamity to turn from your wicked ways into the paths of righteousness, cease your wanderings among wild beasts and devouring serpents, and mollify your minds. Fear not, judgement and forgiveness are at hand! You have all read or heard speak of the retribution visited upon Adam Fuller and John Walker, and upon those that gave them succour; now and on this very day, the same we have heard has overtaken Edmond Denny, a stonemason, but a most ungodly man, who rarely attended his prayers at church, and never wore a woollen cap on holy days, unless found out and fined! A terrible and final judgement has fallen upon him, as it must on all those who do not attempt to douse the fire of their iniquities with the tears of their repentance!'

'I've heard much of this speech before,' says Miss Plesance to Miss Jolly, 'and very tedious that is too! That is part of my father's daily prayers since he came by the Black Dog pamphlet.'

But it seems the majority of those in the square have warmed to the diminutive speaker's words, and by their shouts and calls are ready to begin dousing the fire of their iniquities again by bringing out and exposing Mr Denny's witch of a wife, Mr Flowerdew, or no Mr Flowerdew…

Mr Fleming has worked himself into a fine frenzy now, and exhorts his listeners to shun the ways of the devil, and that the only way to free themselves from the black terror that has befallen them is by rooting out those who thumb their noses at righteousness, the Walkers, the Fullers, and yea, even the Dennys; and taking good counsel from those few pious men in the town, such as certain of the feoffees who were upstanding men of God, and of course, Mr Thomas Belwood, a good Christian man they would all do well to emulate!

There is a great commotion in the surrounding crowd, until Captain Brightwell appears beside Mr Fleming upon the box. We have known the good captain for a few days now and have yet to see him in anything other than a tolerable good humour, even when his patience was being sorely tried by Mr Belwood's brusqueness. But now there are definite signs of anger. It may be the way he brushes away the attentions of Mr Vyner and Mr Costerden, as if they were mere chaff in the wind. Or the manner in which he leaps upon the box, grabs the diminutive reverend gentleman by his jerkin and shakes him till his teeth rattle, before flinging him down into the arms of Mr Belwood.

'None of your viper's poison here!' cries the captain. 'A good man has met his death, and all you can do is attempt to bring further ruin on his poor wife and family! Oh, what a fine Christian gentleman! Make yourself scarce or you will feel the flat of my sword. Be at The Fleece at nine of the clock tomorrow, and a moment late and I will have you arrested!'

Several in the crowd seem to want to protest, but Richard, eyes still blazing, draws his sword and holds it aloft.

'Disperse to your homes! Any man disposed to riot I will have bound and placed in the town jail! Now be gone!'

It has been said that one brave man, full of righteous anger, can turn the hearts of many, and the crowd, who were for a minute or two just now almost a mob, fall quiet and begin to give ground. Much of this movement is down to Richard's words, sword, and force of personality, but not a little is caused by the appearance beside him of Augustyn, grim and angry, and spattered with a good deal of gore. On Richard's other side is Doctor Gordon, the town reeve, looking slightly quizzical, and tugging gently at his sleeve.

'What is it?' says Richard.

'I don't wish to interfere, or anything,' murmurs the reeve, 'but perhaps it's as well I point out that there is no "town jail", as such – in Bongay.'

'No jail!' exclaims Richard. 'Then how are miscreants dealt with and confined?'

'There is a cellar in the castle ruins in which criminals can be locked, before they are taken off to Norwich,' says the doctor, 'but it will not serve more than two or three!'

Fortunately, the townspeople, with the disappearance of the fiery Reverend, and the appearance of Augustyn, are indeed dispersing, and with them the question of overcrowded prison cells. Among the dispersants are Miss Kindred and Miss Poope.

'Well!' says Anna, as they cross the square to Bridge Street. 'I would have it that the expression of anger usually disfigures a man's countenance, but in the case of your captain Brightwell, it seems to lend him even more spirit and animation!'

'He is not "my" Captain Brightwell,' says Cicely, taking an inordinate interest in the stucco mouldings above the door of No. 3 Bridge Street.

'Come, Cicely!' says Anna. 'Was it I, with my not unconsidered charms, who reduced our stern military man, our sharp-minded interrogator, to a drivelling upsetter of inkwells not twenty-four hours since? No, to answer my own question, it was not! It was thee, with just a single look and a barely murmured reply that set the poor captain so!'

'I'm sure I had no such intention!' says Cicely.

'Not with what passes for a conscious mind, I'm sure!' says Anna. 'For a girl of mind and spirit I could sometimes shake you! Love doth not match partners nor sets no tests! His yearning is no fault of yours or his. Tell me you care nothing for him!'

'You speak as if we were in a play,' says Cicely, as they reach her front door. 'Now, no more of this in front of my mother and father.'

As indeed, they are – in a play, not in front of her mother and father, but they have been involved for weeks in writing up the parts for the Holy Trinity Interlude Players in their forthcoming production of "Robin Hoode". But more of this, anon.

TEN

'Mr Molle,' says John Kettle.

Mr Edward Molle is a carpenter, a man of few words and a mournful countenance.

'You will not detain me long, I hope,' says Mr Molle. 'I have a stage to finish building in Trinity churchyard, for the play tomorrow.'

'What did you know of Mr Edmond Denny?' says Richard.

'A godly, truthful man,' says Mr Molle.

'Do you know of any reason why anyone would wish him dead?'

'He was an unexceptional person, who would never offer harm to anybody – not by my knowledge.'

'I have heard from the Rune brothers that you have been much employed with work in St Mary's these last few years?'

Mr Molle's face grows even more mournful.

'That is one way of putting it, certainly,' he says. 'In my first year of business I was employed by the wardens of that church to whiten a tabernacle, then the next year to take the tabernacle down.'

He unships another deep sigh.

'Two years passed, during which I was about my business in other places in peace, when I was paid for making a wooden communion table in St Mary's, as the stone altar was taken down by Mr Pumfret. Then the young king ups and dies, and his papist sister is made queen, and three years after making the table I am to take it down again, and Mr Pumfret he has to put the stone altar back (although it was said it was never quite like the old one) just as that were, and I had to make the rood screen again, and the cross atop, with St Mary and St John painted on it.'

Mr Molle looks so melancholy that John Kettle fears he may begin to weep.

'But all this must have been good for business?' says Richard, trying to be encouraging.

'For business, yes!' says Mr Molle. 'But I am a crafts man, and do not like to tear down what I have spent many days and weeks building up on the whim of a king or a queen or a bishop! In the old times everything was not right, but lasted, that was the same from one generation to another! Now – er, where was I?'

'You'd just put the rood screen back,' says Richard.

'Oh yes,' says Mr Molle, 'and then the queen, she ups and dies, and our good and gracious present sovereign lady is upon us, may she be forever blessed, and the paint is no sooner dry on the screen than I'm ordered to take it down again, and the cross and the rood and everything. And the stone altar is broken down again and the table put back! There ain't no reason to it! People don't know where or whether to wash when they come in the door, who to face, when to kneel and nothin' no more! An' there won't be nothin' left in there at all if that's how we go on!'

'How so?' says Richard.

'Well, not more'n a year ago, there's a notice from your Dean at Norwich ordering the font cover to be taken off, and me to do that, and I did so go in to do it, and there were Mr Fuller and Mr Spiller, the wardens then, with some other men, barring my path, and that the font cover was absolutely not to be removed that or any other day, and I was to be about my business, and Mr Smythe the vicar was there, saying nothing, so I went.'

'Not Mr Adam Fuller?' says John Kettle.

'No, not him,' says Mr Molle. 'His brother Robert, but as alike him in looks and opinion as makes no difference. "Enough is enough," they said, "the church is defaced down to the very stone, and we will brook no more, bishop or no bishop." Not your bishop, Captain, but him that died lately, a much harder, more zealous man, by what all folks say.'

'So the font cover remained?' says Richard. 'I confess I did not notice it within the church yesterday?'

'Oh no, sir,' says Mr Molle, 'I han't reached the end of my story yet. The bishop then summoned Mr Fuller and Mr Spiller to Norwich and did demand them to allow the font cover to be taken down, and any other "remaining ornamentation" as that was written on my letter-of-work.'

'So, the work was done?' says Richard.

'Well, yes,' says Mr Molle, 'amid much muttering and grumbling mind, because of those who favoured the old ways was crazed because that was being done, and those who hated popery didn't think that were going half far enough! I was glad to finish and be out of there, for I'm a Trinity man by family and inclination, and even more so now. But even that weren't enough for the puritanical faction. Now they wanted the screen down itself, and weren't prepared to wait for no order from Norwich, especially as their man had since died and there was our own bishop in now.'

'But the screen remains?' says John Kettle. 'I was admiring it only yesterday.'

'Yes, sir,' said Mr Molle, 'but it was much damaged by two of the church reeves, who kicked in several of the wooden painted panels, and were about to take an axe to the archway when they were discovered.'

'You say church reeves did this thing?' says John Kettle.

'Oh yes, John Mannock and Edward Fielde, stern Puritans both, and the two most vocal in support of tearing down the rood loft and removing the font cover. So they, in their turn, were hauled to Norwich before the bishop, and they got as little sympathy from him as the others had had from the other.'

'They were dismissed?' says Richard.

'They were indeed, for that was not the first time they had broken things in the church, and they were replaced by Mr Spiller, of whom I spoke just lately, and a Mr Thomas Edwards – a shoemaker, see these boots I'm wearing were made by him. And not three months later I'm back in there repairing the screen and making that bigger still! And then there is this dog!'

'You were not at the service on 4th August?' says John Kettle.

'No, as I think I said, I'm a Trinity man,' says Mr Molle, 'But there weren't no dog! No one mentioned a dog 'til that little rag of a preacher brought out his book; and that ain't our dog, that is for certain – you would never find him in a church!'

Mr Molle is almost animated.

'*Your* dog?' says Richard.

'Our dog, Shuck!' says Mr Molle. 'The ghost dog – he ain't mine, that's sure enough, and I hope never to meet him, but from what I've ever heard he's no attender at matins, you're more likely to meet him in the field or march, and hope there's someone with you when you do, lest that's the last you see of anything!'

Mr Molle has become almost cheerful with this thought and, but for the muscles of his face being so out of practice, might have even managed a smile.

Mr Molle says his "God save you's", and clumps off down the stairs.

It does not grow dark until gone nine o'clock at this time of year, and it is past ten when Richard and John Kettle cross St Mary's Street into the churchyard. They are met at the door by Humfry, and by Augustyn and Martin Frye, the tallest man in the town (he all but reaches Augustyn's shoulder) and a blacksmith. They are to remain in the porch to ensure no one else enters. There are two shabby coffins laid on a low trestle in the nave, with candles lit all around them. Doctor Gordon is moving among them, devoid of his robes in a plain linen shift, exhorting a reluctant Ellen to prop up the heads of the two corpses for closer examination.

'Ah, Captain Brightwell and Mr Kettle,' says Doctor Gordon. 'Edmond Denny still lives, but his life hangs by a thread. Please excuse the odour, these men have been in their graves for six weeks, do use these camphor handkerchiefs. Now, this is John Fuller, you will see he has many flesh wounds on his body and arms, but look here – at his neck, and at his black face, and eyes and tongue.'

'If I had not seen his other wounds, I would venture that he had been strangled?' says John Kettle.

'And here also,' says the doctor, 'on Mr Walker, these marks on his throat are of pressure, and here – turn his shoulder to me, Ellen – at his nape, that is not a cut made by any knife or tooth or claw that I know of!'

'But why would anyone want to strangle these men after they had been savaged by this dog – if dog it be?' says Richard. 'We can speak well enough of its efficiency by Mr Denny's remains.'

'I can have no proof of this, as they have lain too long in the ground,' says Doctor Gordon, 'but there is some evidence here that these men have been strangulated, probably by some soft kerchief, so as to leave little markings on the neck. And it is my strong belief, although, as I say, I can have no proof, that they were so killed before they received the other terrible wounds upon their bodies.'

'But where – how?' says John Kettle.

'Where were they killed, and how were their bodies found in the nave? I have no idea! But I fear it may be so!'

Doctor Gordon makes several sketches of the dead men's wounds and lacerations, before ordering the lids to be nailed back on and the coffins reburied.

'Why so many drawings?' says Richard.

'As I say, it is now my belief that these men were unlawfully killed,' says Doctor Gordon, peering closely at his sketch of a long angry gash on Mr Walker's chest, 'and not through the agency of any spectral or supernatural dog. If as town reeve, I am to pursue any unlawful killers through the channels of justice – such as it is, I will be required to produce "evidence" of any claim I make. Should it come to a court of law I cannot present before a justice two decomposed cadavers – but I can show them these detailed drawings, witnessed by your good selves as authentic copies. If you would be pleased to sign your names here, and the date there.'

'But?' says John Kettle.

'No more "buts" tonight,' says Richard. 'Let this grim work be over for now, we will meet with the doctor on a brighter morning.'

'Thank you, good dame!' he says to Ellen. 'This for your work tonight and to buy your strict silence – on pain of prison – until our leaving.'

Richard presses some coins into Ellen's hand.

ELEVEN

It's eight o'clock on a bright sunny morning. Richard and John Kettle are in attendance at the doctor's house, with the drawings spread out on his parlour table.

'I did not say on what premise I based such claims,' goes on the doctor, as if continuing his conversation of the night before. 'Attend here to this wound. The body bears the marks of having being grasped and shaken. Look at the wideness of the rents. You see?'

'I see,' says John Kettle, 'but I still don't understand.'

The doctor calls for his maid and orders her to cross the street to Mr Bryde the butcher and bring back three offcuts of pork, with the fat left on.

'Thank you, Mary, please to place them here on the table – and bring Growler in from the garden, if you would?'

Richard is becoming a little impatient. This is all taking a little longer than he had anticipated, and he is keen to be back at The Fleece and preparing for the advent of the Reverend Fleming at nine o'clock.

'Please bear with us a little longer, Captain,' says the doctor, as Growler makes his entrance. Growler is small and square and black all over, and has pointy ears, shaggy eyebrows, and a short tail.

'What manner of hound is this?' says Richard.

'Five years ago, I made a trip to Caledonia, to the west coast of that land, in search of certain herbs, and one of the natives gave me this creature, then a mere puppy, as a gift.'

'He is very small,' says John Kettle. 'What does he do?'

Growler raises his tousled head and glares at John.

'Apparently these dogs are bred to go down holes after rabbits, but such is their strength they can also account for rats, stoats and weasels, and would make a fox flee. He is of a somewhat dour temperament until he is fed, whence he becomes almost friendly – to those he regards as friendly.'

Growler is still regarding John Kettle as the Reverend Fleming might look upon one of his flock who had been caught with his hand in the collecting bowl.

'I'm sure he's a very fine dog,' says John.

'Now, gentlemen,' says the doctor, 'before us are three chops. I shall offer them in turn to Growler, and I wish you to note how he engages with them.'

Doctor Gordon attaches the first chop to a long pole with a small hook on the end and proffers it to the dog.

'Now, Growler, seize!'

Growler opens his huge red mouth, full of gleaming white fangs, and clamps shut upon the middle of the chop. The doctor holds the pole perfectly still, as the dog pulls from side to side, striving to wrench it free. After a minute or so of this, Doctor Gordon commands Growler to "leave!" and he instantly loosens his grip. The doctor removes the chop and places a second one upon the hook. This time, at the order to "seize" the doctor continually tugs the pole away from Growler, resisting him at every turn, and even pulling the dog off the ground at one point. The doctor retrieves the second chop and places it beside the first.

'There you have it, gentlemen!'

'And the third chop?' says John Kettle.

'Ah, that is Growler's reward!' says Doctor Gordon, tossing the meat to the dog, and ushering it into the garden. 'Now, look closely at the other two, especially at where his teeth have rent the skin.'

'The second is much more ripped and torn than the first,' says Richard, 'but with that one you were not allowing him his way.'

'Precisely,' says the doctor. 'The rips and tears in the flesh are as much my doing by resisting as by Growler's in attacking. But mark, with the first chop, what wounds there be, are enlargements on the first bites, where Growler is trying to worry the meat free from the pole. Now, look at these sketches we took last night of Fuller and Walker's wounds.'

'They are like the first chop,' says Richard, 'but there were many more so on the bodies?'

'If dog it was, it was of a far greater size, and with greater teeth than Growler, and it may have been enraged and therefore more beastly and ravenous. Now, from the evidence of the chop and the sketches, what conclusion would you draw?'

'That the wounds on the bodies of Mr Walker and Fuller suggest that they did not resist the attack of the so-called Black Dog?' says John Kettle.

'That they may have been – dead already?' says Richard.

Richard and John Kettle hurry along Earsham Street, in the shadow of the Castle.

'Loth as I am to disagree with the doctor,' says John Kettle, 'but there cannot be many dogs with greater teeth than Growler! He is not much more than four short legs and a set of great jaws!'

'I would like to see Mr Nicholas Vyner today, as soon after Mr Fleming as may be managed,' says Richard, as they pass through the door of The Fleece. 'Ask Humfry to attend to it, he is to take Augustyn with him, in case a kind invitation is not enough to bring him willingly. On no account bring Simon Costerden – I wish to talk to them separately. Now, John, are you a good Christian gentleman? For your faith and patience are about to be tested to their limits! Bring on the Reverend Fleming!'

Abram Fleming, though rested and restored in his dress to something resembling a man of God, is nothing like as bright as the morning, and appears to have found a fresh subject to be incandescently angry about.

'I have come upon a man, while crossing the churchyard, carrying planks and staves, whom, when I enquired as to his business, first told me to mind my own, but when I persisted, admitted that he was employed in the construction of a final stage against the north wall of yonder church for the performance of a play! Is there no end to the infinite and immeasurable sinnes of these townsfolk? And, I am given further to understand, it is not even to be a play extolling Christian virtues, nor even a superstitious mysterie; but what he was pleased to call a comedie – made for the general amusement of the people!'

The Reverend is so purple in the face that John Kettle, fearing he might have a fit, offers him a glass of water.

Mr Fleming takes a large gulp from the glass and hands it back to John, without thanking him.

'And this in a place reeling from God's righteous wrath, that doth choose to flaunt this frippery in his face, like a whore's ankle to a pious man!'

'I see nothing amiss in a play,' says Richard, 'if it is well done, and of humour, it may raise the spirits of these people, laid low by such recent events.'

'I will not listen to such talk!' yells the Reverend, jumping down from his chair. (He is so small that his feet barely reach the ground when sat upon it.)

Richard, the calmest and most equable of men, is out of patience at last.

'Get back on your chair, sir!' he says, banging the table with his fist. 'And cease your endless ranting. It is twice not twelve hours since I have had to tell you so, and that against a poor innocent man! You will have normal speech with me from this moment, or you will be conversing only with yourself within the confines of the town jail!'

This seems to cow Mr Fleming, at least for the present, and he climbs back upon his perch. He is a man of indeterminate age, anything between twenty-five and forty, with a smooth unlined face, dark eyes and brows, and a plenitude of facial hair, which had once been black but is now flecked with grey.

'Now, sir,' says Richard, 'answer me soberly the following questions: were you at the service in St Mary's on August 4th this year?'

'You know that I was not,' says Fleming sulkily, 'neither have I ever claimed to be.'

'And yet you felt able to give such a detailed account of the event as appears in this pamphlet?'

'If you have read the preface, you will note that I wrote down the order in which I received the story, and which was grounded upon truth.'

'Correct me, sir,' says John Kettle, 'your knowledge in these matters may be greater than mine; but is "grounded" not another word for "based"?'

'It may be so,' mumbles Fleming, who seems not much interested in this line of questioning.

'From whom did you receive the story?' says Richard.

'From diverse among those who were present.'

'Is this your first visit to the town?'

'I have not been here before.'

'So, these "diverse among those present" came to you, sought you out?' says Richard.

'A small number of people from Bongay were in London on other business and came to see me – yes.'

'How so?' says Richard. 'What drew them to you?'

'I am known as a writer of tracts and have been engaged on a History of England for some years past, so they may have thought the story of some interest to me – as indeed it was.'

'Was Mr Belwood among their number?'

'You know it to be so, and others of the town's council, Mr Towtinge, Mountell, Grime, and some others.'

'And you believed sufficient of their account to rush it into pamphlet form?' says Richard.

'There was no rush,' says Fleming. 'A topickal pamphlet is of no use even a year after the event it describes, this happened more than six weeks ago. And I had no reason to disbelieve the testament of such sober Christian gentlemen.'

'Yet the wardens in their book speak of the church tower being struck by lightning, and Mr Walker and Mr Fuller being killed there, and no mention of a dog?'

'There is much confusion of accounts during such a dark and terrible tempest as beset Bongay on that day,' says Fleming. 'Such as to make no man's recollection one that can be truly verified – only before God. I believe you have found it so among the townspeople?'

This is a new side to Mr Fleming, calm, rational and reasoning in his speech, but with the slightly insufferable air of someone dealing with a persistently backward child.

'What we have found will be made known in due course,' says Richard. 'It is to be hoped after some rational thought and deliberation.'

This last sally was totally lost on the reverend gentleman, to whom wit was only the word "with" with the "h" left off.

'I have one final question for the present,' says Richard, '…of a theological nature. If, as you claim in your pamphlet, the visitation of the Black Dog was a sign of God's wrath against the sins of his people, why would he use this dog, which you describe as "the devil in such a likenesse" as an instrument of his anger; and how can you, as a Christian minister, countenance such a use?'

The calm, rational, reasonable Reverend Fleming disappears in an instant, to be replaced by the foam-flecked ranter.

'If you had taken the time to read my preface, it states clearly that the power of the Prince of Darkness is allowed through God's permission and sufferance to be sometimes used to correct and to punish! You, to question me, in a town where every second dwelling is an alehouse, where women walk freely abroad without company, where the word of the Lord is taken in vain, where wild games are allowed in the street, and lewd caperings in the churchyard, you—!'

Richard bangs the table again.

'Mr Fleming, our interview is at an end. You are to remain in the town until you are given permission to leave, and you are to refrain from any preaching or raising of the populace during that time. There is the door, sir.'

TWELVE

'The play's the thing!' says Cornelius. 'And some weather, of course! But it looks set fair for the rest of the week.'

He is sitting on the edge of the recently erected stage with his brother Thomas.

'It was good of the doctor to allow it so, in view of recent events,' says Thomas.

'He is a master of physick, and of panaceas,' says Cornelius. 'And what better panacea for spooks, murder and ghostly dogs than a merry tale of olde England?'

Mr Molle appears before them, looking as if he has just received news of a recent bereavement.

'Sirs, the stage is all but completed, and Miss Poope and Miss Kindred are begun on the scenery and stage boards. I will be about my other business. Good day!'

'If I could write a tragedie, it would feature Mr Molle,' says Cornelius, as the carpenter trudged back to the town. 'He would not need to speak, one glance at the audience would convey all the world's sorrow in an instant.'

'And yet his wife is a sprightly dame, and he is father to four children,' says Thomas.

'Look, brother, here is Master Gallant again, yearning for a part, no doubt he has heard of Edmond's accident, and hopes to fill his shoes.'

'He could play a corner of the stage had we not four already,' says Cornelius. 'He is wooden enough.'

'I fear his mind is not altogether on his acting,' says Thomas.

'There has been no evidence yet of "acting" to animate his mind,' says Cornelius.

'I meant he was as concerned to be near Miss Poope, whom he knows is much about and behind the scenes.'

'Perhaps we should pay her to always be before him,' says Cornelius. 'And then what roles he could play: Troilus to her Criseyde, Dante to her Beatrice!'

'Robin to her Marian?' says Thomas.

'No, this is supposed to be a "merry" play and he too speaks always as if at a graveside. Anyway, I dare not risk a woman on the stage – only think what Belwood, Towtinge and Grime would make of that! Good day, Master Gallant, yes, we were all alarmed to hear of Mr Denny's misfortune, and no, we do not know how he does! Robin Hood, you say? Of course, I should have thought of you, but I am afraid the part is taken – I have asked Captain Brightwell to take the role! Perhaps you would consent to play a "merry man"?'

'I didn't know you'd asked the captain to be in our play?' says Thomas, as they watch Mr Gallant disappear into the distance. Every few yards he stops and gives out a hearty laugh, and slaps himself on the thigh, as the Rune brothers had assured him that Merry Men were in a more or less constant state of amusement, and it was as well he got himself into the role.

'I haven't,' says Cornelius, 'that is where we're going now.'

'But even if he says "yes", how will he learn his words in two days?'

'He doesn't have a lot to speak,' says Cornelius. 'Nothing that can't all be written down on the back of his sleeve. And we know he can wave a sword around and get the attention of the womenfolk. He's made for the part!'

'What about his other business here?' says Thomas.

'It is only for two hours on an afternoon, with a little practise today and tomorrow! You would think him grateful for some time away from that stuffy room, asking questions of baker's wives and solid citizens. Oh, and I want Augustyn for "Little John".'

'He has no speech at all!'

'And Little John has but three in the whole play! We'll stand a voice behind the curtain to say his lines.'

'But Nick Vyner was to play "Little John". He will not be best pleased.'

'As I've said before, brother; the play's the thing, not the actors in it. He'll just have to be pleased to be a Merry Man again, along with Master Gallant. We only gave him the part for his skill with a quarter-staff! Even with his boots built up he was less than an inch above the rest of us! Do you think I can put Robin Hood and Little John on the stage with a seven-foot giant watching from the audience? We'd be jeered from the parish!'

Today is not a good day for Nicholas Vyner. He has spent the early part of the morning at Mr Belwood's house attending to the many and various needs of the Reverend Fleming and his breakfast, who seems to be dissatisfied with everything that is brought to him and sends a deal of it back to the kitchen. Then on his way to be interviewed by Captain Brightwell, he meets the Rune brothers in the street, where Cornelius regretfully but firmly informs him that he will not be required for the part of Little John in the forthcoming play, but he may seek out Master Gallant for some sharp lessons in being a Merry Man. Mr Vyner begins to remonstrate, and damns all Merry Men, whereupon he is sternly reminded by Cornelius that: "The play's the thing, and that it is taking part that is important."

'Who then has replaced me?' says Nick.

'You will know soon enough,' says Cornelius. 'Do you know the saying: "When one door closes, another door opens"?'

'I have heard it,' says Mr Vyner. 'What of it?'

'Well, that's the only clue you're getting! Go away and think on it.'

Thus, Nick finds himself languishing in the taproom of The Fleece, under the disapproving eye of Mr Mellendyne, while first the Rune brothers and then a posse of feoffees claim precedence over his interview in the upper room.

'I am sorry to importune you when so busy, Captain,' says Cornelius, who has knocked and entered the upper room before Richard has time to say, 'Who is there?'

'I know you have a busy day, but I wanted to ask you if you would join us in our play of Robin Hood in the churchyard on Saturday. Poor Mr Denny was to have played Robin Hood himself but he is – er?'

'More dead than alive,' says Richard. 'I have played in the Mysteries at school and church but never on a publick stage in a serious—'

'Oh no, this is a comedy,' says Cornelius. 'And truly, there are not many lines for you to say, here is a script which I can leave you – it will require a brief rehearsal today and tomorrow, not half an hour each, and may be some diversion from all the dark business you have been about.'

John Kettle is not the only one to have noticed the lines of care and weariness on the captain's face.

'He'll do it,' says John Kettle. 'Leave the script here, Master Rune, we – he shall look it over during our dinner.'

'Oh, one more indulgence. We would very much like Mr Flowerdew to play the part of Little John, if you and he are willing. I know what you will say – but he does not need speech, we will make him a voice.'

'Mr Flowerdew will be delighted, we're sure,' says John Kettle. 'Although Humfry will be most slighted.'

'There are never too many of the Merry Men,' says Cornelius. 'We meet in the inn-yard here at six o'clock. Good day!'

No sooner have they closed the door than it is opened by Mr Towtinge and Mr Grime, who without preamble or politeness demand to know whether Mr Walker and Mr Fuller have been taken from their graves; when and where Mr Denny is to be buried, and why it is that vile and scandalous plays are to be allowed to be performed near God's holy house?

'As to your first, they have been taken out and put back, and we have learnt much from their examination,' says Richard. 'You may tell Mr Belwood so. As to Mr Denny, what leads you to believe he is dead? Who has said he is dead? As to your third, what is so vile about a folk tale most of us first heard from our mother? And I am told Trinity has oft been used for plays and mysteries! And furthermore, I am to be in it! Now begone!'

'There is little enough that is free in this world to give us joy,' says Richard. 'Yet there are always pinched, mean men like those and their ilk who would try and deny it to all!'

'So, you will play Robin Hood?' says John Kettle.

'Of course!' says Richard. 'What makes you think I would not? "Down with the Sheriff of Nottingham! Long live King Richard!"'

John Kettle is pleased to see so much new animation in the captain; it was almost as if he had invited the feoffees here himself, on purpose.

Mr Vyner's bad morning is almost at an end. He is receiving a thorough grilling from Captain Brightwell. The captain wants to know where Mr Vyner was during the latter part of the football match, and also during the hours before the discovery of Mr Denny.

'I was at Mr Belwood's house, at my work, and he will vouch for my appearance on both occasions.'

This answer sounds a little too rehearsed to the captain, but he keeps his own counsel for now, and like a good soldier, switches the point of his attack.

'Were you at the service on August 4th?' says Richard.

'Mr Belwood is a good Christian gentleman, and ensures that every member of his household attends divine service as he does.'

'So that is a "yes"?' says Richard.

'If you have it so,' says Nick Vyner.

'Where were you sitting?'

'At the back, near the porch door, behind Mr Belwood.'

'So, you saw the dog run down the church?'

'I did, and I saw it savage the papists, and wring their worthless necks as it passed.'

'Please show some respect when you talk of the dead!' says Richard. 'Now explain to me – how can a dog, of whatever size or nature, wring a man's neck by merely passing him by?'

'I know not how,' says Mr Vyner sullenly. 'I only know what I saw. It was as it said in that book.'

He points at Fleming's pamphlet on the table. He cannot help but notice the script lying by it with "The Tale of Robyn Hoode" written on the front page. He cannot help himself.

'Are you to be in this play?' says Nick.

'I am asking the questions!' says Richard sternly. 'That will be all for the nonce, Mr Vyner. I may say that I am not satisfied with any of your answers. Yes, I am in the play, in the part of Robin Hood.'

Again, Nick Vyner cannot help himself.

'But not that of Little John?'

'No, Mr Flowerdew is to play Little John,' says Richard.

Which just about makes Mr Vyner's morning. And there sits Augustyn, downstairs in the taproom, playing a friendly game of dice with Mr Foweler. Mr Vyner, fists clenched, takes a step towards him, before recalling their last encounter in this place, and his aerial re-entry into the street. He carefully opens the door so as to leave his escape clear, plants his feet apart in the doorway, arms akimbo, and yells out, 'Little John! Ha! Pshaw! Humbugge!'

Augustyn looks around, mildly surprised.

'Now, what was all that about?' says Mr Foweler. 'Two sixes and my pot, I think.'

THIRTEEN

Richard and John are to Doctor Gordon's house. They are surprised to find a large, open-sided tent in the garden. The doctor is seated at a small table beside it, chopping and mixing fresh herbs.

'Ah, gentlemen, good day to you! I have some good news. Mr Denny still lives, and I have reason to hope he may yet make a recovery.'

This is good news indeed, to the captain, who had fully expected to hear that Mr Denny had died in the night.

'Indeed, he might have died,' says the doctor, 'and might yet! I think the fact that he was found so quickly, and his wounds cleaned straight away and pressed with great mullein may give us some cause for hope.'

'May we see him?' says Richard. 'Is he conscious?'

'Indeed! He is here beside us, lying in a bed in this tent. I am a great believer in "fresh air" as an aid to healing, rather than being confined in a dark room full of bad humours. I had the servants carry him out this morning.'

Mr Denny is awake and even manages a wan smile for the captain. He is lying in the tent upon a pallet under a light blanket. His arms and legs are bandaged, as is his head and throat.

'Edmond has a strong constitution, but pray do not tax him with many questions,' says the doctor.

'I only wish to give thanks that he is alive,' says Richard, 'and to wish him whole and hale once more.'

'There was a dog,' whispers Edmond. 'A great, black, dog, with black eyes, and a rank stench.'

'Do not distress yourself,' says Richard. 'There will be time enough to talk of dogs when you are well again.'

'It was called away,' says Edmond. 'It was called hither! Who can call Black Shuck!'

Mr Denny is looking somewhat distressed and is given a cordial by Doctor Gordon.

'Enough, Edmond,' says the doctor soothingly. 'The captain is only here to ask after your health today. You must lie quiet and under my command if you are to be well. Look, here is your wife come to sit with you!'

'It has been his constant refrain through the night,' says the doctor, as they walked through to the street, 'that there was a dog, and it was called away.'

John Kettle says little but misses nothing and, as they walk back to The Fleece, reminds the captain of the blackness of the dog's eyes.

'What of it?' says Richard.

'When you told me of the creature on the common, you spoke of its red eyes.'

'That I did,' says the captain. 'Fortunately I was never close enough to that beast to know if it had "rank breath".'

'And even allowing for some delirium brought on by his wounds, it is interesting that Edmond recalls a human voice calling away his attacker. In all the many accounts I have heard and read since we have been in this place, there has been no mention of any companion.'

'John, I'm aware that a secret is only a secret in this town until the thought is breathed out, but I wish to keep Mr Denny's condition as close as we possibly can for now. The doctor will keep it so as a matter of course, and Mrs Denny and children are in his house and safekeeping, but it might suit our purpose if the rest of Bongay thinks him dead for now, or very near death. Tell Humfry the same and convey it to Augustyn, he is fond of Mr Denny, I think. I shall swear the Rune brothers to this secret, as it will make their entertainment all the lighter.'

'How so, Captain?' says John.

'They were concerned that putting on a play so soon after a death, and that the death of the actor to play Robin Hood himself, might not be in the best spirit.'

'They are both men of good spirit,' says John Kettle.

'Oh, and on no account let this be known to Moses, another man of good spirit, but one with a tongue which might outrun the Black Dog himself across a bare field.'

'He is master of the town's busiest inn, so may know of it already,' says John.

'Then sit down with him and fish for what he knows,' says Richard. 'If he does know, silence him by my order, and quell his curiosity if he does not.'

Richard has never been to a rehearsal before, and knows little of the ways of players, but in his youth he attended inn-yards and churchyard ales where mysteries and comedies were put on, and half-remembers going with his mother to see Robin Hood outside a church in Petersfield when he was ten years old.

Augustyn is already at the inn-yard, practising with a quarter-staff.

'G'day, Cap'n,' says Humfry. 'As you can see, Little John is primed and rarin' to go.'

'He is aware that this is only a play?' says Richard, looking a little apprehensive as Augustyn cracks an imaginary opponent on the head with the tip of his staff, before swinging it around and catching another with a blow between the legs.

'Ouch!' says Humfry. 'It's as well that was not for real! Yes, Captain, he knows it's but a play, and I think from his reaction that he has acted in some before. I used some pictures of Robin Hood and play-acted a bit myself, and it took a bit of time, but now he points at Robin Hood, and salutes, which is you, and then at Little John and himself, so I think we've more than met it! After that, I think I could play him myself!'

'Except you would be "Very Little John",' says John Kettle, 'a "Tiny John", and we would all need a spyglass to see you on the stage!'

It appears Humfry is to play the part of "Very Little John" after all, as the Rune brothers have asked him to stand behind the stage curtain and provide a voice for Augustyn.

Cornelius Rune greets them warmly and informs Richard that they will rehearse two scenes today: Robin Hood's first meeting with Little John on the banks of a woodland stream, and his ambush of the Sheriff of Nottingham and Maid Marian in the forest. Thomas has laid a long plank down in the yard, and Augustyn stands at one end, with Richard at the other.

'Here are your words, Captain,' says Thomas. 'Speak here, after my brother, who, as the narrator, says:

"Now Robin Hood, down by the river,

Spies a great giant, coming hither."'

'How now, fellow. Yes, you, great ass, down from the bridge and let me pass?' says Richard.

'Ye-es,' says Cornelius, 'that was tolerable, but was a good deal too polite. Recall that you are Robin Hood, rightful Earl of Locksley, and are used to command and to be obeyed, as indeed you are as a captain! Do not request him to get down but order him!'

'How now, fellow! Yes, you! Get down from the bridge and let me pass!'

'I shall not!' says Humfry in his very deepest voice. 'I was on here first!'

Augustyn scowls, grips his quarter-staff and shakes it in a menacing manner.

'Get down!' says Richard, un-slinging his bow, and aiming an arrow at him. 'Or I shall make my point with this shaft.'

'I have only a stave,' says Humfry. 'A true knight would offer a fair fight.'

Richard leaps off the plank and looks around.

'Here!' says Thomas Rune. 'I am a thicket! Reach your hand in here!'

He hands Richard a stave with two or three twigs still attached.

'Strip them off as if you had found it so!' whispers the thicket.

Richard pulls the twigs from the stave and stands back upon the plank.

'I'll not be stopt with that little stick!' cries Humfry, as Augustyn advances to the middle of the plank.

Humfry and Cornelius have given Augustyn careful lessons about mock fighting, how to swing the quarter-staff with full force, yet stay it just before contact so it looks to the audience like a full-blooded blow. They have need to try this a few times before Augustyn gets the idea and Humfry some sore ribs from being sent flying about the yard.

'I'm glad this is only "mock fighting",' he wheezes, rubbing his midriff. 'I'd hate to see you when you was really angry.'

According to Richard's script, he is to fall back before Augustyn's first onslaught, counter with such force that his attacker is almost forced off his end of the plank, then be gradually driven back towards the middle before taking a round arm swing at the giant, which he ducks under, before sweeping Richard's feet away and depositing him in the stream. Everything goes very well until the final moment, when Augustyn forgets to pull back, Richard leaves a leg in the way and receives a powerful blow on the shin.

'Ah – ooh!' says Richard, rolling around in the blue blanket that serves as the river.

"And so, the mighty Robin Hood,
Is dumped and doused in the flood."

'Yes, that seems to have gone well,' says Cornelius. 'I don't think we need to do it again?'

'Ooh – aah!' says Richard, hobbling to his feet, and hopping to a bench.

'No? Good!' says Cornelius. 'Then on to the next scene! Bernard here, is to play the evil Sheriff and young Tom Goode is to be Maid Marian, and Edward Shue his maidservant, but they are both apprenticed to Mr Acle and are thatching a roof in St James today. But Miss Cicely and Miss Anna have agreed to stand in just for the rehearsal.'

Upon hearing the words "Miss Cicely" the captain is so startled he throws out his arms, which tips over the bench, and deposits him on his back.

He looks up into the beaming face of Mr Bernard Curdye.

'My, but you're a one for flinging himself about!' says Bernard, hauling Richard to his feet.

'I am more flung about than flinging!' gasps Richard.

'Now!' says Cornelius. 'Attend! Here is the Sheriff of Nottingham, with Lady Marian and her servant woman, and a guard, riding through Sherwood Forest when they are accosted by Robin Hood and several of his men. Bernard, would you not grin so much, you are a foul, fell, Sheriff, such as would cut off a man's ears for hearing your business and think nought of it, or slay one of your servants for not anticipating your every wish?'

'Oh dear!' says Bernard. 'I fear I will fail as the Sheriff; I can never cut a splinter without fainting, and don't normally know my own wish 'til after the servant has done it!'

'This is a play,' says Cornelius, 'and you are not yourself in a play.'

Richard tries to keep that thought about "not being yourself in a play" firmly in the front of his mind during the next few minutes of rehearsal with Miss Cicely Kindred.

'Now, Captain,' says Cornelius, 'you are not to say much, you are desperately attracted to comely Maid Marian here, but you must convey this to the audience through longing looks and sighs, while you, Marian, remain properly demure, but are to take the part of the Sheriff at first, he is after all, your uncle. You, Anna are Beth, Marian's faithful maidservant, and you are very short with the outlaws, and especially Robin, until you realise he means your lady no harm. Also, you see their mutual attraction before they do themselves!'

'And they say a play cannot imitate life!' murmurs Anna.

The scene is got through twice, the first time with a great deal of stumbling and missing of lines by the captain, but the second much more smoothly. Richard has most difficulty with the final lines, where he takes his leave of Maid Marian before she is escorted from the forest.

'Take her hand – just so!' says Cornelius. 'Look into her eyes thus! You wish her a safe journey, but your hand and your eyes wish for so much more!'

'I – I wish you a safe journey home – and that we would meet again,' stammers Richard.

'He stumbles with two "i"s and gazes upon her with two more!' says Beth.

'That is not in the script, but will be hence, for it is a fine pun,' says Cornelius.

'I do not know how it will be so?' says Maid Marian. 'Are you to waylay me in the forest again?'

'Wherever your way lies hence,' says Robin Hood, 'I would wish to lay in it.'

'A pretty sentiment, and well put!' says Cornelius. 'And thus the audience will be prepared for the archery competition, and Robin being drawn into Nottingham and the Sheriff's clutches. This we will rehearse tomorrow, along with Robin's escape and final fight with the evil Sheriff.'

FOURTEEN

And now to a great encounter. In a tale concerning a black dog, you are probably thinking we have seen little enough of the creature itself, save at the beginning, whence he came, as it were, bounding onto the scene. Since when we have had only glimpses, and rumours and hearsay, and where the dog has been, but no dog himself. There has been Growler, certainly, a small black dog and fierce enough when roused, but of a size to make you fear more for your ankles than your throat. And there is nothing of the spectral or ethereal about Growler, he is firmly and four-square of this earth. There he is now, trotting purposefully through the gate of the doctor's house, after his evening exercise.

Further down the street, just before the bridge to Earsham, a man is sitting outside a ramshackle alehouse painting a sign. On this sign there is a white lightning bolt over which a black dog is jumping. Above this image are appearing the words "The Blak Dogge Inn". The Blak Dogge Inn has, up until today, always been known as "The Spotted Cow" (and is no more an inn than I am an alchemist), a name to which it will return tomorrow when a posse of furious feoffees happen upon the alehouse keeper, a Mr Thomas Snedden, and get him to take the sign down. What was he thinking of? Does he wish to draw more of God's wrath down upon the town? In truth, Mr Snedden was not thinking at all beyond attracting more passing customers into his alehouse, by exciting their interest in a bit of topical and interesting news and, as for that, according to this pamphlet, which he'd had his brother read out to him, the Black Dog was an instrument of the Almighty, so where's the harm in drawing attention to 'im?

This piece of gymnastic theological thinking left our four feoffees flummoxed for a few moments, until Mr Towtinge and Mr Grime remembered a by-law which decreed an alehouse keeper had to give a week's notice of a change in name, which then had to be approved in council. So take the sign down now, if you please!

Richard walks alone on the mounds below the castle ruins in the early evening. Half of his mind is puzzling over the remarks of Edmond Denny this morning, while the other half is more pleasantly engaged in attempting to memorise his lines as Robin Hood, and recalling exactly the sound of Miss Kindred's voice as she asked whether she might be waylaid in the forest once more?

The captain sits down upon a low wall, and gazes over the ruined keep at the sun just beginning to set. He makes a valiant effort and places Robin Hood and Maid Marian in the back of his mind. Mr Edmond Denny said three things this morning. The dog that attacked him had black eyes, it had a rank smell about it, and it was "called away". There is a faint rustle in the long grass about him. Richard looks up and espies a pair of long, pointed, black ears about ten yards distant. The ears bob up and down for a moment then hop off in the direction of the castle keep.

'Aha!' says Richard. 'The "Chicken Rabbit", if my eyes do not mistake me!'

The rabbit stops when twenty yards distant and turns back towards Richard. The captain rises from the wall and follows but keeps his distance. The rabbit leads Richard under the shadow of the castle wall and then is seen no more. He is about to scour the long grass with his sword when some light rubble, dislodged from above, bounces off his shoulder. Richard looks up and takes a sharp intake of breath. It is the woman. The figure he had seen beneath the tree on the common, but now silhouetted above him on the keep tower. Richard is looking about for a door to the tower when a voice hails him.

'Captain Brightwell! You are to come this moment to the Moot Hall! Doctor Gordon has found something in the cellar! You must come now!'

'Why would he send you?' says Richard.

It is a keen question, for the messenger is Symon Costerden, the servant of Mr Belwood.

'I was all that was about at the time,' says Symon. 'Now you are to come quick, or all may be lost, the doctor said.'

Richard looks again at the ruined tower, but the dark woman has vanished into the twilight. As they reach the gate into the town, Symon is squashed by a squealing hog that appears from the bushes and attempts to squeeze through the narrow space at the same instant.

'Begone, or I will flitch you here a whole month early!' snarls Symon, drawing his dagger and pricking the pig about the neck. 'Now, Captain, be quick and follow me.'

The door of the Moot Hall is open.

'The doctor is down those stairs,' says Costerden. 'He's along the passage.'

At the bottom there is a long, low brick tunnel, lit along its length by two torches. Symon has followed Richard down the stairs.

'Take my torch,' says Symon. 'He's at the end of the passage; he said he's found something to do with that devil dog you're all looking for.'

The passage is very dark, and Richard can see no sign of the doctor at the end of it. He runs softly along the tunnel for more than a hundred yards, until it opens up into a cavernous space.

'Doctor?' calls out Richard, holding the torch above him. There is no response. Richard can hear the sound of running water, such as is made by a small stream running over stones. Richard rubs his eyes, which are watering in the gloom, and looks again. Two flickering points of light appear before him in the darkness. Richard feels the cold prick of fear on his skin. There is the sound of pads on wet stone, of a groan that seems to come up from the depths of the earth itself, and two points of light that seem to shimmer and glow as they grow ever larger. He rubs his streaming eyes again. Is that a flash of red, or is it a trick of his sight, such as you have after looking at the sun too long and closing your eyes suddenly? Richard makes to pull out his dagger with his left hand, which gets caught up in his doublet. He cannot say exactly what manner of creature this is, it is black, certainly, and of great dimension and very hairy, and in the half-light of the torch he can see it running towards him, and there can be no doubt now, a pair of great, gleaming red eyes! The dagger is still nestling somewhere in his attire, and he has no room to draw his sword, so he can do no more than cross his arms and place them before him as the beast is upon him. Richard falls on his back, half in and half out of the stream. There is no click of jaws, no ripping of sinew, no spurt of blood, no tearing of flesh. Or rather there is, but it is all going on behind Richard in the mouth of the tunnel. He staggers to his feet and out of the stream. The only thing he can see is the flickering light of the torch, lying a few feet away. There is the most tremendous sound of a struggle going on before him. Richard picks up the torch, and holds it before him, but all that can be seen is a yelping, snarling mass of black, which rolls to and fro across the cavern, and to the very edge of the stream, at which point one of the creatures lets out an unearthly, spine-tingling scream and leaps away from the water, while the other attempts to reach across and sever Richard's arm, the click of its massive jaws missing him by an inch. Richard backs away from the water to the far wall of the cavern, as far away from the creatures as he can manage. The struggle lasts another five minutes, before one of the beasts breaks off suddenly and races off down the tunnel, yelping piteously. Richard quickly douses the torch, and stands completely still, breathing as lightly as possible. It is not completely dark in the cavern now, or his eyes have become more accustomed to the gloom, and he can make out a large black shape, snuffling along the edge of the stream. Richards exhales a little too abruptly and the dog raises its head and looks directly at him. Even in the darkness, Richard can clearly see the red gleam in its eyes. He sighs, deeply and loudly, as he draws his sword and dagger. There is no point in concealment now. The beast growls, at first no more than a whisper but growing in volume and intensity with every passing second. Its red eyes begin to glow in the darkness. Richard has probably been spending too much time in the company of actors, because he has an irresistible desire to shout out, "Begone, foul beast!" Instead, it is another voice that gives them both pause, from far away, beyond the stairs at the tunnel mouth.

'Captain Brightwell! Where are you? Is there anybody about?'

The dog turns its head, listening intently, and then bounds off down the passage.

'I am here!' croaks Richard. 'Through the tunnel! But mind you the dog!'

There is the sound of a door being thrown upon its hinges, and several feet scuffling in the darkness. A flaming torch appears, and beneath it the concerned faces of John Kettle and Humfry.

'Sir?' says John. 'Are you safe?'

'Are you safe, John, did you not meet anything in the passage?'

'Some bats flew in our hair as we opened the door, sir,' says Humfry, 'but otherwise nothing.'

'You are sure?' says Richard.

'Well, it ain't a very wide, spacious tunnel,' says Humfry, 'so I think we'd have noticed anything trying to squeeze past us!'

'And any other?' says Richard.

'Any other what?' says Humfry.

'Any other creature!' says Richard. 'There were two beasts down here, not three minutes hence, fighting for their very lives, with me as the winner's prize, and they now seem to have both vanished into the very ether!'

'Ye-es,' says John Kettle, glancing keenly at his master as they emerged from the stairwell into the sunlight. 'Two creatures, you say?'

'And don't look at me like that!' says Richard. 'Two great black beasts, snarling and biting great pieces from one another. There ought to be a trail of gore from here greater than that of Mr Denny, but I see there is… is…'

'Nothing,' says John, quietly. 'We came along the street from the South Gate, so have seen this front door these last ten minutes, and no one has passed out nor in but ourselves.'

'So, I imagined it all?' says Richard. 'I am off my head, am I? Like the dog and the dark lady on the common over again?'

'No one would say so,' says John Kettle, 'at least, not here. It is just that we were not with you when you saw these things, and they have left...'

'Not a rack behind!' says Humfry, who was walking behind them.

Richard and John Kettle both turn and look at him.

'Sorry!' says Humfry. 'I heard that in a play somewhere.'

'I tell you,' says Richard, 'and I am completely in my right mind saying this, that I saw two – two, mark you – very large dog-like creatures in that cellar, and that, had not one of them been there, I would now be in a condition similar to that of poor Mr Bowtell, or Mr Denny. No more questions now, both of you, I need to work out in my own mind what this means. I must pay the town reeve a brief visit, so you to The Fleece and collect Augustyn, then proceed to Mr Belwood's and demand on my authority the custody of Mr Costerden. You are to use force if necessary!'

FIFTEEN

Mr Denny is much improved this evening and is sitting in a chair outside Doctor Gordon's back door. Doctor Gordon does not seem very surprised to hear of two black dogs.

'It might help to explain how this dog is apparently capable of being in two places at once – at once in the belfry and running about the church, and in answer to your question, no, I have had no dealing with Mr Symon Costerden today or any other day, so his late summons to you was entirely false, and evidently a ruse to draw you into great danger.'

'But why were they fighting each other?'

'Perhaps they were fighting over you,' says the doctor. 'Perhaps you were their dinner!'

This last remark even raises a weak smile from Mr Denny. Richard sighs deeply. It is proving difficult, first with John Kettle and Humfry, and now with the doctor and Mr Denny, to explain how it had felt down in that cellar. There had been fear, and excitement, and dread, certainly, but Richard retained another very strong feeling that he could not convey to anyone else. That the two creatures who had fought so savagely in front of him had been of a different order – from each other, and that he had been very, very fortunate that the struggle had ended as it did.

'And there is the question of where the dogs went to,' says Richard. 'It was a narrow passage, and stair, and Humfry and John saw no one or thing pass out, yet I assure you, two dogs, or large creatures the size of calves, disappeared without a trace.'

Mr Costerden is nowhere to be found, says the servant girl at Mr Belwood's, surprised by callers at this late hour. Neither does she know the whereabouts of her master or Mr Fleming. They went out some while ago and said nothing as to where they were going. Mr Vyner is also nowhere to be found. And no, as far as she knows, there is, and never have been no dog, and she's never seen one, leastways, not in the house, and she don't go into the grounds much, but she'd not seen one there, either; there was a cat, a ginger one, belonged to one of the grooms, but no dog. She'd heard a dog once, howling; over behind the Castle Hill, but never seen one – well, of course, she'd seen a dog, everyone's seen a dog, but not ever in this house...

'Enough!' says John Kettle, putting up his hand. 'Thank you, you must have your work to do, and we must be going.'

'If she don't work as she talks, she must have *all* her work still to do,' says Humfry.

Richard is not surprised to hear Symon Costerden has flown but is interested in hearing more of what the servant girl has to say.

'Which puts you in a minority of one!' says John Kettle. 'An interview with her will make Mrs Jekell seem like a nun under a vow of silence!'

'No matter, I still wish to speak with her,' says Richard. 'Sometimes it is possible to pluck a gold coin from a swirl of leaves.'

'One rehearsal, and our captain begins to speak like a travelling player!' murmurs Humfry.

Mr Mellendyne appears with a tray of ale. He is looking mildly conspiratorial. He squeezes onto the edge of a settle beside Augustyn.

'Good sirs!' says Moses. 'I have heard of your canine encounter next door, Cap'n, and am relieved to see you so well.'

Richard has now been in Bongay long enough not even to enquire how Mr Mellendyne could have known of such a thing.

'Er – thank you,' says Richard.

'I've no idea whether what I am to say is of any mind,' says Moses, 'but I have heard,' here he pauses greatly for the effect, and pulls the end of his nose about prodigiously, as if he had been listening through his nose, rather than the usual aural organs, 'I have heard, that Mr Belwood and several of the feoffees are meeting in secret at The Falcon this night to plan how to put a stop to the play to be performed on Saturday.'

Humfry, who has been quietly sipping his ale, stands up at this juncture and, requesting leave of the captain to continue his reconnaissance of other inns, departs with Augustyn in tow. We shall go with them, as the captain has had enough excitement for one day, and we, if Humfry still has his wits about him, may learn something.

Upon entering The Falcon, they are greeted with derision, until the locals focus their bleary eyes, and Augustyn is identified, whereupon an unnatural quietness descends upon the taproom. It only takes a few moments of offhand questioning of the ill-favoured pot-boy to ascertain that Mr Strine is at a meeting in the next room with Mr Belwood and some other gentlemen, although that is not quite how the pot-boy, a lad of limited and rather coarse vocabulary, describes them. The pot-boy knows this, because he has just this moment delivered several bottles of ale and wine with glasses to the room, and has been given strict instructions that they are not to be disturbed for the next hour.

'And how did you deliver the refreshments to the – er – gentlemen?' says Humfry.

'Why, through that hatch at the end of the corridor,' says the pot-boy, in the half-second before he is coshed by Humfry and dragged into obscurity behind some ale barrels.

'Now, Gus, and don't look at me in that way, it is only a cosh, and he shall have no more than a headache,' whispers Humfry. 'We have been enough days in The Fleece for you to know what to do should any of these denizens ask for ale in the next-half hour! I am going to listen at yonder hatch, and I must not be disturbed!'

Humfry carefully and quietly props the hatch a few inches open and sits beneath it, couching a glass of Mr Strine's finest ale.

'It is all amiss! The captain lives, and the beast is sore scratched!'

'How can this be?'

'I know not, but the dog is much torn about, and Thomas at The Fleece said that Brightwell is as if unharmed.'

'Will the dog be able to perform again in two days?'

'I have treated its wounds quickly and well.'

'I am not easy in my mind with this venture, anymore! You swore there would be no deaths, and there have been four to this day, near five, and now more violence planned.'

'Saturday will see an end of it, thence we will be cleansed and purged of this evil.'

'And you will be several times richer!'

'We will *all* be of benefit, you as well! You must hold your nerves and your tongues for but two more days. Now you know what is expected of you. You must all be seen in the churchyard, supporting the man of God in his outrage—'

'We are all good men of God I hope, and will not have to feign "outrage" at such a spectacle as that promises to be! It shall come from our hearts!'

'That is very well, just so you keep their attention up until the play begins. You, meanwhile, will take the dog along Falcon meadow, on the west bank of the river, where you will not be seen, and into the back of Bridge Street. When he is recovered, you must kill him quickly, tie stones around his neck and drop him in the middle of the river!'

'It seems a cruel end for such service.'

'You, I suppose, would make a pet, a lapdog of it? You would not long have a lap with such a hound in the house! It must be done as I have said, there must be nothing to link us to this tale. We will have gained everything we wanted, and our "devil-dog" can pass into legend and story, and be seen no more, except by those in their cups.'

Humfry thinks he has heard enough, and creeps silently back to the taproom. The pot-boy is rising groggily from behind the barrels, rubbing his head.

'You do get some rough fellows in here!' says Humfry. 'We chased the ruffian who felled you up the street but lost him in the square. Now you might oblige us with two pots of ale. Here comes your master, we will say nothing of what has occurred to him. He might take a dim view of you lying about among the barrels with the room untended. We don't wish you in any trouble!'

Mr Strine looks mildly discomfited at Humfry and Augustyn's appearance in his alehouse, greets them guardedly, says little while they sup their ale and watches them carefully to the door.

'Wot news for the captain,' says Humfry, as they return up Bridge Street. 'Mr Strine was one of those voices, and Mr Belwood another, and there is no mistaking Mr Towtinge's foghorn!'

He reaches up and slaps Augustyn heartily on the back. 'We have 'em!'

SIXTEEN

'Well, not quite!' says John Kettle. 'We now know what we only suspected before, that we are not dealing with a spectre, but we have no proof – they can simply deny everything. We could arrest them all today, but on what charge, and with what evidence? And you can be sure none of the men in that room will be bloodying his own hands with the dog, so whoever is to be attacked on Saturday may still be in great danger, even if all the plotters were somehow squeezed into the town jail.'

'We know he lives in Bridge Street,' says Humfry.

'Half the quality in the town live in Bridge Street,' says John. 'At least eight of the feoffees, by my reckoning, and we don't even know if it's a feoffee that they are after.'

'I want everything to go ahead as normal,' says Richard. 'We will rehearse the play as planned tomorrow. I am to ride to Ditchingham in the morning to see Lady Sherborne. John, a word with you in my room, before we turn in.'

Captain Brightwell has just finished his breakfast and is preparing to saddle his horse when he is accosted by a plump, smiling lady.

'Captain! Begging your pardon on interrupting your business, but I'm given to understand you are making a visit to Sherborn Manor this morning.'

The captain sighs inwardly. He supposes he might put a board outside the door of The Fleece early each morning, with all his engagements for the day set upon it, but even that would be a waste of time and effort, as these psychic citizens seem to know his intentions before he has formed them himself.

'I am to visit there,' says Richard, rather swayed by the brilliant smile, which he feels he has seen somewhere before, but not attached to this lady. 'How may I be of service?'

'I wonder if you might give this letter to Mr Bernard Curdye, Lady Sherborne's steward? He is my husband, and a fine man but somewhat forgetful, and I have made a list of things he must remember on his return home tomorrow.'

The fleeting mystery of the smile is solved, it is a mirror image of her husband, Bernard's, whom Richard encountered on his first visit to Ditchingham. Richard tries to picture life in the Curdye household, with the relentlessly cheerful smiles of the parents, and no doubt a legion of children with rictus-like grins plastered to their little faces, all being determinedly happy. Richard likes balance and harmony in his world, and mentally pairs off Mrs Curdye with John Kettle, his sober countenance and serious mind would offset her incessant cheeriness and provide the children with a little relief from all the jollity. Or his own rather rumpled visage across the table from the smooth dark hair and bottomless eyes of Miss Cicely Kindred…

'Er – Captain?' Mrs Curdye gently touches his sleeve. 'The letter?'

Richard is recalled thus from his reverie and, reading the name of the steward above the seal, recalls his last conversation with him.

'Mrs Curdye?' says Richard. 'There is something your husband said when we last met that concerns you. I wonder if I could ask you of it?'

'Ask away!' says Mrs Curdye. 'I employ such good girls that the stall will sell itself!'

'Mr Curdye told me that you had seen the Black Dog as a girl, but had come to no harm?'

'Yes, that is so – although my grandmother then upped and died – but she was eighty-five! Oh, that's the other thing I wanted to speak with you of – funny how things rush through so and make you forget, it's the busy lives we lead, I'm always saying to Bernard, so much to think about, the business, the children, what to have for dinner, oh, any number of things to be thought about, and only the hours awake to think them, unless you're dreaming, of course, but I never can remember dreaming, can you? And Bernard says, in that case how do I know I was dreaming? Yes, I've seen him again, twice!'

Richard had been attempting to break back into the conversation for so long that he almost misses her purpose when it eventually comes.

'Your pardon, seen who again?'

'Three days since, the day before you came into the town, I was walking back across Castle Meadow with my washing and I came upon him on the path. That didn't seem to come from nowhere, that was just there. Stopped and looked at me with those great, gleaming red eyes, just like when I was a girl. But I weren't afraid, he didn't do me no harm that time, so why would he hurt me now? He's got the longest legs of any dog I ever see. You – well, not you, you're tall, but most anyone else could walk under him if'n they bobbed their heads a little. I stood as still as I could, like you do around wild animals, and I never said a word, and he walked around me twice and then sort of leapt into the long meadow grass and was gone!'

Richard is still trying to imagine what it must feel like being around Mrs Curdye when she is not saying a word, when he realises she has paused for breath.

'You said you have seen him twice?' says Richard. 'When was the other time?'

'Just yesterday,' says Susan. 'Although I didn't exactly see him then but felt him.'

'Felt him?' says Richard.

'Yes, I should have said before, whenever he is about the air do turn uncommon cold as if that were a February wind, and I was out the back of the Moot Hall yesterday leying the buck, quite late in the day, but 'twas still warm and sunny, and that's warm work, when my very back prickled with cold and raised all goosebumps on the back of my neck, and I turned and saw a black shadow by the gate. That weren't no dog, but everything else was bright and colourful, but there was this black shape moving in and around the gate. I was a bit scared by that, I will concede.'

'What was it about?'

'I know not!' says Mrs Curdye. 'That was there for more than a minute, just sort of draped over the gate, almost as if that were wore out? Then it just melted away into the lane.'

Richard thinks much on Mrs Curdye's words as he trots his horse down Bridge Street and makes for the lane to Ditchingham. She might rattle on at a pace hard to keep up with, but she is a woman of intelligence and discernment, and obviously has some other quality that drew whatever this phantom dog was to her; but without seeming to arouse its baser instincts.

Lady Sherborne is in her high-backed wooden chair, in a sunny window bay, as if she has never left it since his previous visit.

'I don't leave it often,' she says, taking his hand in greeting. 'They won't let me go far, or do anything, but sit here and be waited on. They come and read to me when they can, but the days can be very long. I understand from Bernard that there is to be a play, and that you are to be in it?'

'I have been cajoled into being "Robin Hood" by the Rune brothers, in place of Mr Denny, who has been sorely injured.'

'Yes, I have heard it so. Mr Denny is a fine craftsman, and an honest man. But it is said he was savaged by the dog that you seek?'

'He has been savaged certainly, and we do seek a dog – it is that which prompted my visit.'

Richard tells Lady Sherborne all that they knew of Mr Belwood, Reverend Fleming, the feoffees and the killer dog.

'You must be very careful of Mr Belwood,' says Lady Sherborne. 'You have not been in Bongay many days, but you will know now how quickly gossip spreads, and secrets are unravelled, so it will not be many hours until he knows that you know of his designs.'

'Of that I am only too well aware,' says Richard. 'We know that he and his cohorts plan another attack on a dwelling in Bridge Street during the play tomorrow, but we do not yet know who or where.'

'Mr Belwood and Mr Graygoose are antagonists of long standing,' says Lady Sherborne. 'They were once partners in matters of business and property but fell out some years ago. I believe Mr Graygoose to be an honourable sort of man. It is said he did not care anymore for Mr Belwood's conduct, especially over the eviction of tenants. They have been in dispute over certain outstanding properties from that day to this. I was asked to arbitrate between them several years ago but found it beyond my Christian patience. Belwood is as devious as a snake, and Graygoose is as stubborn as stone. But Edward Graygoose will allow things to languish if he is let, while Belwood will neither forgive nor forget.'

'And where?' says Richard.

'He lives – or he did the last time I was with him, in a large house just the river side of The Chequers alehouse.'

'Mr Hemline is also no friend of Mr Belwood, they do not see eye to eye in matters of faith. Hemline is a bit of a recusant and has been fined several times and, he believes, rightly or wrongly, that Belwood has informed against him. He lives three doors above The Falcon, on the left.'

Richard carefully drew a little map of Bridge Street and marked "Graygoose" and "Hemline" upon it.

'Oh, and we must not forget Pewter Mulso, our town clerk, you have not met him yet? Mr Belwood is often at daggers drawn with him. Pewter has fined him time without number over his care – or lack of care – of his livestock, which he tends to let run wild and trample over other people's property. I had forgot him, they have no liking for each other at all. He lives five houses below The Queen at the top of the Street.'

Richard cannot help but wonder that Lady Sherborne plots all her geography of the town by the alehouses and inns within it.

'And this spring he fell out for a short time with Josiah Kindred, so Bernard tells me, something about his son and Kindred's daughter?'

Richard snaps his quill and blots his note-paper.

'Belwood has a son?'

'Oh yes, a great oaf of a lad, Bernard says, spends most of his days lying beneath tables in alehouses and terrifying milkmaids. It's said he had designs on Cicely Kindred, or rather her dowry; but Josiah told him "no," and he shortly afterward left for London. Mr Kindred lives at—'

'I know where she – he, lives,' says Richard quickly.

'I was going to say he lives at home quietly with his wife and daughter,' says Lady Sherborne. 'Well, good day to you, Captain Brightwell, I hope to see you at the play tomorrow. I will attend if the weather stays fine, Bernard shall drive me. I shall probably not enjoy it, but I must make what amusement I can in my remaining days.'

Richard's horse is able to please himself on the way back to Bongay, and often stops to partake of a tussock of grass here, and a sip in the stream there, such is the distraction of the man upon his back. Richard had meant to use the time deciding on the most likely victim of Mr Belwood's attentions, but having all but dismissed the probable threat to Mr Kindred over such a small matter, he cannot help dwelling on Lady Sherborne's allusion to Miss Cicely Kindred. She had not said anything about Cicely's feelings towards – this oaf, this charlatan, this wastrel – only that her father had refused him. What if that means she harbours some tender feelings for the detestable brute? What if she is even now counting the days since he left for London and is pining for his return? It is at this point that Richard notices his horse has left the path and is wading into the river.

'I have been a-sick visiting, this morning,' says John Kettle as they cross St Mary's Street, bathed in the early afternoon sunshine.

'I have called upon Mr Denny, who is coming on by degrees. He is a good man with a good mind. We spoke much of his work and the many people he has to deal with. He said some interesting things about our Mr Belwood. He says Mr Belwood has posed himself as a champion of reform only so that he may benefit from the travails of others. And since the Act was passed, he has received several acres confiscated from those whom he has denounced as recusants. Mr Denny thinks that, far from satisfying his greed for land and property, this "good fortune" has only served to increase it.'

'Lady Sherborne has just told me Belwood has a son?' says Richard.

'Oh yes, Mr Denny spoke of him as being the beneficiary of some of his father's newly acquired property. Edmond has no very great opinion of him, he is a well-formed youth, very conscious of his good fortune, who gives himself airs even over his father, and whose predilection for young women is only matched by his aversion to any form of useful work.'

'But who is presently in London?' says Richard.

'Yes, so I believe, there was a tryst with some woman of the town,' says John Kettle, 'that made his remaining here impossible.'

By his offhand manner it is plain to Richard that John does not know the identity of "some woman of the town", and that Mr Denny did not know either, or chose not to tell him of it. Why would Mr Denny choose not to tell of it? Did he know that it would discomfit the captain? That it was common knowledge in Bongay that Cicely Kindred had lost her heart to the melting glances and clean limbs of – Richard is aware that he does not even know the sneaking viper's name! Walter, or Francis, or something preening, like Orlando. Yes, Orlando Belwood, in his tight doublet and bright hose, drawing sighs and swoons from all the shallow young maids of Bongay, chief among them the capricious young Cicely Kindred…

'I recall,' says John Kettle, 'he's another "Thomas", which should come as no surprise, given his father's self-regard.'

'Good day, Captain, Mr Kettle.'

It is Miss Poope and the flighty minx Kindred, walking arm in arm across the church path.

'I am afraid you must suffer us upon the stage again today,' says Anna. 'We have just heard Edward and Tom cannot be spared. Let us hope their memories are as good as their thatching!'

Until two hours ago, the news that he was once again to act opposite Cicely would have produced the usual joyous commotion in Richard's head and heart, but now that he has convinced himself that she is a shallow flirt pining with love for a preening popinjay with a dubious taste in clothes and a scoundrel for a father; Richard affects a look of studied unconcern which borders on disdain.

Miss Poope, who misses nothing, enquires if the captain is quite himself today?

'I am well, thank you,' he says, stiffly.

'That is good to hear,' says Anna. 'I am well, and I believe Cicely is also in the best of health?'

The captain, thus forced into some sort of acknowledgement of her companion, manages a grunt and a nod in Miss Kindred's direction, before striding ahead.

'Ladies!' says John Kettle, looking both bemused and embarrassed. 'We have had a very busy morning.'

'Indeed!' says Anna, ignoring Cicely who is tugging at her sleeve, imploring her to be quiet. 'So busy that the captain has not time enough to exchange the time of day, it seems!'

This last sally brings Richard to his senses, for a time at least, and he turns, apologises for his distraction, and greets both young women most effusively, almost too effusively, as if he has come upon them for the first time this morning, instead of just two minutes ago. He asks after Josiah and Mrs Kindred's health, and Cicely's siblings (she has but a brother), and anyone else attached to the family?

A slight frown creases Miss Kindred's fair brow.

'Anyone else attached to the family?' she repeats. 'What – what do you mean, sir?'

'Any friend, living far away, whom you might wish closer?'

Richard cannot help himself. He is spouting gibberish again. Cicely is looking upset and slightly offended by his tone. The captain ploughs on.

'I meant, oh, excuse me, I do not know what I mean!'

The captain strides off again across the grass. John shrugs his shoulders at the ladies, bows and hurries after his master.

'Your swain is in a strange humour today?' says Anna.

'He is not "my swain"!' says Cicely, crossly.

'What can he mean about "a friend living away, whom you might wish closer"?' says Anna. 'I'm at a loss to know his mind.'

'I begin to wonder if he has one,' says Cicely. 'Good day, Mr Curdye, and Susan!'

Susan Curdye has been a good friend to Cicely since she was a small girl.

'We are all going to the same place, I think,' says Anna. 'We were just wondering why the captain is so out of sorts with Cicely today.'

'Ah!' beams Bernard. 'He is "out of sorts with Miss Cicely", you say? I think I may know why that might be?'

'Well?' says Mrs Curdye.

'My dear?' says Bernard.

'Tell us!' says Mrs Curdye.

'Oh – ah, yes, well, and this may not be the reason – but Lady Sherborne said—'

'Are you quite well, Captain?' says John Kettle, on catching up his master.

'Yes,' says Richard, 'why do you ask?'

'Oh, nothing! But you were somewhat abrupt with the young ladies just now and I thought—'

'Abrupt?' says Richard. 'I simply asked a perfectly reasonable question – which any maid of sense and understanding – ah, but she is so flighty!'

'Come, sir! Collect yourself! Miss Kindred, flighty?'

Richard comes very close to wagging his finger in John Kettle's face.

'You don't know the smallest part of it! Beneath that well-formed, pure-looking exterior—'

Here they are interrupted by Cornelius Rune, appearing from behind the stage and shaking them both by the hand.

'Good day, Captain, and Master Kettle, and here are other members of our company approaching! I would like to take yesterday's scenes first.'

Cornelius and Thomas are at the edge of the stage. They are watching the scene where Robin takes his leave of Marian.

'I – I mean, I wish you a safe journey home, and that we would meet again,' drones Richard, in a flat monotone.

'He stumbles with two "i"s and gazes upon her with two more!' says Anna. 'Only he does not! Where did "I mean" spring from? And why cannot he look her in the eye, as he did yesterday?'

'I do not know how it will be so!' says Cicely, dropping the captain's hand as if he had the plague. 'Are you to waylay me in the forest again?!'

'Yesterday's invitation sounds today like a threat or a challenge,' murmurs Thomas.

'Wherever your way lies hence,' intones Richard, staring straight over Cicely's head, 'I would wish to lay in it.'

'His tone is so sepulchral that "her way" might be his grave,' says Thomas.

'There is something amiss here!' says Cornelius. 'All her animation of yesterday has turned to animus, and his delivery is more wooden than the staff he carries.'

'We will have to hope our two young thatchers spark more allure tomorrow,' says Thomas.

The archery competition does not go too well either. Bernard does a fine turn as the evil Sheriff, gloating when he spots Robin Hood among the aspirant archers, and teasing Maid Marian as to her favourite.

'That well-formed fellow over there,' says Bernard, beaming like the sun on a May morning, 'is he not a fine archer?'

'Any yeoman can fire an arrow!' says Cicely.

'Those are not the words I have here,' mutters Cornelius.

Richard takes aim before the target. He is to look at Marian, who is to give him a brief smile of encouragement. Instead he receives a thunderous scowl, which so discomfits him that his first arrow misses the target altogether and grazes the posterior of one of the stage-hands.

'We had better have that again,' says Cornelius, 'as Marian's response is to be: "A fine shot, such as I never have seen."'

'His aim is like to his heart,' says Cicely to Anna, but in a voice loud enough for Richard to hear. 'Both wounding and wayward.'

Richard's next arrow flies true to the centre of the bullseye.

'That is more a reflection of *my* heart,' says Richard, stiffly, 'straight, unwavering, and true.'

Maid Marian is to present the silver arrow to the winner on a velvet cushion.

'Take your prize!' says Cicely, thrusting the cushion at Richard so abruptly that the arrow flies off and downwards at such a force as to spike his foot. John bends down quickly and extracts the shaft, while Richard hops about the stage on one leg, shouting, 'Ow, ouch, Ow!'

The idlers gathering to watch think this is the best part of the play so far, and laugh heartily, and jeer the unfortunate archer.

'Perhaps we should leave it in,' says Thomas. 'It hath caused more merriment than any other trick, so far this day.'

'No, it would make a nonsense of the plot,' says Cornelius, 'and a cripple of the poor captain. Come, he is in some pain, let's go to him.'

The captain is helped back to The Fleece by Augustyn, who picks him up as if he were a baby and carries back across the churchyard. John Kettle is left to stand in as Robin Hood.

Mr Mellendyne is all of a flutter on their return.

'Captain Brightwell – you are injured! Quick, Gus, bring him into the back. Fetch water and a poultice; was this the work of the dog?'

'No, sir,' says Humfry, 'this was the work of a maiden, play-acting in a play!'

'I like to watch them,' says Mr Mellendyne, 'but I'm not sure I altogether hold with play-acting. There's all them trapdoors to fall through, and balconies to topple off, and smoke, and swords and suchlike, and arrows of course.'

Richard's pierced foot is cleansed and bandaged, and he is made to sit and rest and is plied with pasties and ale, so the day does not end so badly. Excepting there is no word or note or sign or sight of Miss Cicely Kindred. Cicely is a young woman of much more spirit than we have previously seen and, indeed, is not aware that she has injured the captain so. At the moment of handing Richard the cushion she sees that Tom Goode has arrived, who is to play Maid Marian, and feeling both angry at the captain for his behaviour, and a slighted sense of mortification that she is needed no longer, she makes as if to leave the stage. She is aware that Richard is hopping about on one leg, but so he was yesterday, after being so sweetly struck by Augustyn. Her passion for the play has gone for the day, and she walks slowly home with Anna. Who is thinking of how best to lightly suggest that they might put their head in the door of her uncle, Mr Mellendyne, to ask after Richard?

The very mention of his name fires Cicely as if from a cannon.

'How he could think such a thing of me?' says Cicely. 'And he hardly knowing me!'

'You – we don't know that he does think such a thing of you,' says Anna. 'We only know what Bernard thinks he overheard Lady Sherborne saying concerning you.'

'Then why treat me so?' says Cicely. 'With such looks and dull disdain in his voice?'

'I would not fret,' says Anna. 'He shows every sign of one who is thinking of you a great deal, almost to his distraction. That some swain would think so of me!'

SEVENTEEN

At noon the next day, the town reeve and the Rune brothers are standing in front of the stage.

'We have made a dais over there,' says Cornelius, 'with a canopy and chair for Lady Sherborne.'

'We look to be blessed with good weather,' says Doctor Gordon. 'Perhaps Providence threw down all its thunderbolts in August and has now relented.'

They are approached by Mr Molle.

'The canopy over the stage is erected and garlanded,' says Mr Molle, as if announcing the death of a near and dear one, 'and the trapdoor is tested and does not fail.'

'We are grateful to you, Mr Molle,' says Thomas. 'You will stay and see the play?'

'It is a comedy, I believe?' says Mr Molle, looking more

miserable than ever. 'I may stay, I can be as merry as the next man. I like a good laugh.'

'The actors will have done their job more than well if they raise a smile on that visage,' says Cornelius.

A crowd begins to gather in the churchyard. Today is a holy day and whole families are streaming in across the grass, appearing in the lanes from their cottages, a wagon full of Ditchingham Dames slowly ascends Bridge Street, men emerge from The Fleece, The King's Head, The Chequers, rubbing their eyes in the bright sunlight after the dimness of the taproom. And what is this? A group of soberly dressed men, gathered by the church gate. One among them ascends upon a box and begins to speak to the passing throng.

'It seems not everyone is for your play,' says Doctor Gordon. 'It appears to be our brave pamphleteer and his patron, plus the reforming members of the town council.'

'A dark puddle of disapproval in a swirling sea of approbation!' says Cornelius. 'As the poet said, although no one seems to be paying them much mind.'

'They will not be bothered by that,' murmurs the doctor. 'I think their sole purpose is to be seen in public and together.'

'For what purpose are we given these holy days?' thunders the Reverend Fleming, for it was he upon the box. 'It is to spend them in prayers and contemplation of our manifold sins and wickedness, on our knees begging our Almighty Lord's forgiveness, not sprawled on some ale-soaked greensward among doxies and harlots!'

A large muscle-bound maltster shoves his iron-jawed, grizzled face up close to Abram Fleming's.

'Ooo you calling "Anne Arlot"?' he growls.

'Pardon, sir,' says Abram, 'you mistook me.'

'If me and the missus, and the seven – ent' issue,' here he waves an expansive arm to indicate his myriad children, 'choose to see a bit of a play, I don't see no harm in it, and neither does 'immup there I warrant!'

After delivery of this muscular piece of theology, the maltster spits at Fleming's feet and moves on. That pious gentleman waits until he and his clan are a safe distance away, before continuing his harangue, as if nothing has happened. His cold, grey eyes light upon Captain Brightwell, John Kettle, Humfry and Augustyn emerging from The Fleece and crossing the street to the gate.

'And if example were needed!' bellows the diminutive cleric. 'Here it cometh now. Those sent – or so we are led to believe – by a bishop, to make good matters of religion, instead spend their days – when they are not pestering good townsfolk who would be better about their business than answering tiresome questions about that which is obvious to all! – instead, I say, spend their days drinking and carousing at football, and not only attend vile revels such as this play, but consent to act in the same!'

Richard, John and Humfry pass by without a word or gesture, having heard much of all this more than once. Augustyn lingers behind, hands on hips, the frown on his brow deepening with every wave of Fleming's arm.

'He cannot understand a word he's saying,' says Humfry, 'but Gus does not seem to care for the Reverend Fleming.'

As the others turned to look back, Augustyn stretches out his right hand and grasps Fleming firmly by the throat, raising him several inches from his box. While holding him aloft, he carefully stamps on the Reverend's box, smashing it to matchwood, before placing the choking cleric gently down upon the remains.

'As eloquent a response as I have ever seen,' says John Kettle.

The churchyard is filling up with all manner of people, all trying to get a good view of the stage. Some sit along the town wall, others on grass hummocks, and many gather in the standing room beneath the stage. It is a warm day for mid-September, and those looking for relief sit in the shade at Augustyn's feet, who is enjoying the variety of local talent which precedes "Robin Hood: A Tale of Old England". There is a juggler who cannot juggle, a jester with no jokes, a squeaking orator, and several singers who cannot sing. Augustyn cheers them all lustily. Cornelius has gathered his company behind the stage.

'Gentlemen, we are assembled,' says Cornelius, 'for the purposes of this performance; we are to be called "The Staithe Men", and so I shall call us in the prologue. Richard, these are Tom and Edward, who are to play Marian and Beth?'

Tom and Edward are made up as maidens, and look tolerable enough, if not looked at too closely, being both fresh-faced, handsome youths of sixteen.

'We have been rehearsing our parts across the roof of St. James' farmhouse this past week,' pipes Tom, 'and my mother and sister have been instructing us both in feminine ways!'

For the moment, Richard is just pleased that they are not Miss Kindred and Miss Poope. He is nervous enough about appearing before the crowd, now almost filling the churchyard.

'Are they used to plays and players much, in Bongay?' he says to Thomas Rune.

'Oh yes, we've had proper players from Norwich, and Bury here before, the Queen's Men came here once – although they were only passing through and did not perform anything. They like a bit of blood, and a lot of laughter, and if we don't provide it up on the stage, then they do it themselves.'

'How so?' says Richard, nervously.

'Well, one company came a year back, calling themselves "The Essex Men", though it turned out they weren't The Earl of Essex's Men, they were just men from Essex. When they got on up on stage here, they said they was "The New Men of God," and we thought they might be going to give us one of the old York or Chester plays. But no, they stood up there like so many Abram Flemings and started denouncing our town, our church and our revelry, and our play-acting! It wasn't long before a few root vegetables began landing among them, and then much worse, 'til they left in a body heading for the South Gate and the safety of Essex!'

There is now so much noise and bustle in the churchyard, that Richard wonders how they are to ever capture the audience's attention. A tent and tables have been rigged up by Mr Mellendyne and is selling copious quantities of ale, there are other stalls selling chops and nuts, and pedlars hiring out cushions for a penny. After much good conversation and four or five cups of ale, the maltster and several of his friends and fellow maltsters feel an overwhelming need to express themselves in dance. This results in a deal of good-natured stumbling about, accompanied by raucous singing, which is just beginning to turn into a version of "Why Are We Waiting?" when one of the maltsters' progeny accidentally tramples upon a supine feoffee, a supporter of the Belwood interest. This slightly injured worthy, whom we instantly recognise as Mr Towtinge, leaps quickly to his feet, and strikes the clumsy youth several times about the head and shoulders.

'Oy, yew!' yells his enraged parent and protector, rolling up his sleeves as he falls upon the flailing feoffee. A spirited rumpus ensues. Not quite on the scale of the recent game of football, but a very fine melee, nonetheless. Mr Belwood had planned to bring a large group of followers into the churchyard at this point, to advance upon the stage and cause sufficient disruption to halt the proceedings. Instead, this fresh column find themselves engaged in a pitched battle with some very angry maltsters and their friends and relatives.

'I'll say this for Bongay,' says Humfry, climbing upon the stage for a better look. 'In truth, I was not looking forward to coming here, but there's something going on every minute! Is that not Mr Grime over there, taking wing over the church wall? This is not at all the sleepy little town I took it for!'

'I think,' says Doctor Gordon, 'that it is time for some diversion from this end of the playground, while the "sleepy little town" still stands.'

Martin Frye advances to the edge of the stage.

'Good folk of Bongay,

The Staithe Men are here,

We bring you a play!'

As well as being the tallest man in Bongay, Martin is also possessed of the loudest voice, a stentorian roar that rattles window frames and ripples tiles upon the street roofs. If you had been strolling on the far bend of the river, in Ditchingham, you would have heard his echo on the water, and mistook it for a distant rumble of thunder. The fighting stops in an instant, as that corner of the churchyard turns as one towards the stage.

'That is begun!' says the maltster, releasing his hold on Nicholas Vyner's throat (who was having another bad day, and wished no more to be associated with plays and with acting). 'Come, let us get nearer to see the play!'

There as a general drift towards the stage, except from Mr Belwood's men, who are now in no condition to march anywhere, most being senseless, supine and draped over mounds.

'A tale of old England,
Of righting of wrongs,
Of outlaws and sheriffs
Of valour, and songs!
There dwells in the greenwood,
An outlaw most bold,
And this is his story,
As oft has been told…'

'Come, that was well said!' says Cornelius, shaking Martin's huge hand as he came behind the curtain. 'And hath certainly gripped their attention!'

The play goes very well from the beginning, and the audience do not seem to object to Richard as Robin Hood, so far. Bernard makes a fine Sheriff, no trace of a grin upon his grim visage, and earns many boos and cat-calls for swindling Robin of Locksley of his lands and driving him into the forest. Lady Sherborne, swathed in rugs and seated high upon her dais, appears to be much amused by her faithful steward acting a foul villain.

'I enjoyed the brawl just now,' she says to Susan Curdye, 'and thought it might be better than the play, but Bernard is making us a splendid rogue.'

The fight with Little John is a triumph. The previous evening, in the gathering gloom of The Fleece's yard, Richard and Augustyn had gone through the sequence for over an hour. It had become a kind of dance, and Gus had attained a kind of fleet-footed grace that completely belied his size. After the painful early rehearsals, they had learnt to deal seemingly hard blows with their staves which barely brushed the skin. Today they race and spin back and forth across the plank, ducking, jumping and feinting as the crowd roar them on. As they near the last flourish and blow, Richard cannot help but think the end will be something of a let down as he falls in-stage onto the soft blue blankets that are to represent the river. But he has reckoned without the Rune brothers, who never see a play but they see a way to improve its effects. So as Richard topples off the plank, the blue blankets disappear, the yawning trapdoor opens, and he falls with an almighty splash into a cattle-trough, filled with water, which Cornelius has had carefully positioned beneath. The effect is stupendous. Richard, soaked and gasping for air, struggles to his feet. The audience cheer him to the steeples as Augustyn pulls him back onto the stage.

'And so, the mighty Robin Hood Is dumped and doused in the flood!' cries Cornelius.

'Quick, Captain, behind here!' says Thomas. 'We have you a dry suit of Lincoln green all prepared!'

'I am sorry for your soaking,' says Cornelius, as Richard peels off his costume, 'but you may not have fallen in that natural manner if you knew what lay beneath you.'

Richard had heard it said that the life of a player was one of surprise and danger, and here was the truth of it, especially if the Rune brothers were managing proceedings.

One street away, Mr Josiah Kindred is dozing in his chambers. His wife and daughter are at the play. He does not much care for play-acting himself, but he has no objection to others enjoying it. He is wearied by the attitude of some of his fellow feoffees, who seem suspicious of any form of pleasure or diversion. One of them, Mr Towtinge he seems to recall, actually suggested that he go and stand by the church gate with others and harangue that part of the populace that was attending the play! That the ancient office of feoffee should come to this! And Mr Towtinge could not guarantee that the awful bearded ranter Fleming would not be present, indeed, he seemed to think Mr Fleming's presence an additional attraction! Josiah puts his feet upon the fender, reclines further into his chair, and stifles a great yawn. Mr Towtinge is a strict young Puritan gentleman, with no family but his own parents, so as of yet can have no appreciation of an empty house, of a wife and children safely at the play, and no noise except for the gentle hubbub of the players and audience way beyond the church wall, and the sleepy quacking of the ducks on the river. It is a warm afternoon, and Mr Kindred has left the back door open. He begins to doze.

He awakes with a shiver. There is someone standing in the doorway. Josiah rubs the sleep from his eyes and rises from his chair. It is a figure in a dark shawl, looking out into the yard. Some beggar woman must have got into his garden.

'Take thyself off!' croaks Josiah, still not properly awake. 'Begone! No alms here!'

Mr Kindred is usually of a gentle, generous disposition, and always gives alms to the poor, but they normally knock, or are passing his front door, and the sudden appearance of a supplicant in his own yard and garden has somewhat discomfited him. The more so in that she pays him no attention whatsoever.

'W-woman?' says Mr Kindred, more awake now and beginning to feel just a little afraid of this strange figure. 'What are you about?'

Without turning her head, she motions him with her right arm back to his chair. Josiah suddenly feels a great chill in all his limbs, and a trickle of icy sweat down his backbone. The woman sits on a bench near the door in his kitchen, her back to the wooden table. Mr Kindred returns to his chair, not in any way relaxed now, and wishing he had gone to the play.

Mr Nicholas Vyner has had enough. As soon as this day is done, he is finished. He is off to London for some peace and quiet. Mr Belwood was a bad enough master before all this dog business, but now all these "dreams of avarice with a dog" have made him impossible, and dangerous. Still, today will see an end to it. He emerges from the tunnel into the charnel fields below Holy Trinity, carefully replacing the round wooden cover, and covering it with bracken and branches. He can hear the noise of the play and the shouts of the protesters and the audience over the church wall above him. He keeps to the narrow path along the base of the mound, screened from the fields by a row of elder bushes. The creature pulls and heaves, but Nicholas has made sure it is safely muzzled and muffled. There is one bad moment near the riverbank, when a rabbit hops into view, and his arms are near torn from their sockets, but here they are at The Backs, unseen and unheard. He removes the muzzle, ties up the beast securely, and checks the contents of his satchel. Two documents to sign, full name and dated, and then five minutes with the door shut where Mr Kindred will meet his maker, and the dog get some much-needed exercise. Even Nick Vyner thinks this a bit harsh, given that he is to promise the man his life if he signs, and then be made to kill him anyway. Not "kill him", he reminds himself, just leave them alone in the room together. Still, this is the very last time, he is then to dispose of the dog in the river, the stones are prepared there by the fence, in a sack. He slides quietly through the yard-gate, and pads quickly up to the back door.

The crowd in the churchyard are on their feet. Robin Hood has escaped after winning the silver arrow, but Maid Marian has been captured by the evil Sheriff and sentenced to death. Will Robin reach her in time?

'Har!' says the evil Sheriff, standing in the middle of the stage with his legs astraddle and his hands on his hips. A storm of booing greets this exclamation. Bernard is greatly enjoying himself. He leers at the crowd.

'Har, har har, harr! A pretty young teasel to dangle before the outlaw! D'you think that enough to tempt him?'

'No!' yells the crowd.

'Then we have no end to our play!'

'Yes!' yells the crowd.

'And he will come sneaking and snivelling, in shadows and corners, like a serpent,' says the Sheriff. 'Afraid to meet an h'officer of the law in open, manly combat!'

Here Robin appears at the back of the stage, a finger to his lips.

'Ssssshhhh!' says the crowd.

'Why shush?' says the Sheriff. 'There is none but I here, am I not enough to fill a stage? Hark, what is that, a bat squeaks!'

He turns suddenly, but Robin shadows behind him, and remains unseen.

'I thought I caught a flash of Lincoln green,' says the Sheriff, 'but mayhap – it must have been a trick of the light. What say you?'

Robin is by his shoulder, his sword at the ready.

'He's behind you!' chorus the crowd.

'Nay, he is not!' calls the Sheriff.

'Oh, yes he is!' yells the crowd. Robin pricks the Sheriff's rump with the point of his sword. The crowd are near delirious. A great sword fight ensues, with the Sheriff engaging in many comic falls and asides before he is finally run through. He takes an age to die, clutching the hilt of Robin's sword to his bosom.

'Aaaah!' says Bernard, sinking to his knees. 'I am pricked and punctured, like a pin in a bladder, my life, my twisted days are strait at last and ebb away.'

'That is very fine,' says Cornelius, 'and not writ here! Copy it down, Thomas.'

'Our expiring officer grows lyrical in his demise,' says Thomas. 'Listen, there is more!'

Bernard rises on his elbow.

'Ah me, thy faces grow dim as shadows, wouldst that all the ill I've done be undone! I die!'

He slumps to the floor, and the crowd give warm applause. He makes as if to rise again.

'Bernard!' hisses Cornelius. 'Pray you stay expired. They will not stand for a further resurrection!'

Robin rushes over to Marian, loosens her bonds and folds her in an embrace.

'I did not think Tom Goode such a tall fellow,' says Anna Poope. 'His Maid is near as tall as our outlaw.'

Cicely will not admit to noticing the captain at all today, besides allowing that he appears "a little cramped".

'More than a little,' says Anna. 'Why, it may be the green hose, but his legs are like spindles.'

It is at this moment the scream is heard. A high, keening screech, that rips the soft evening air like a sharp, serrated knife though velvet, and lasts a full ten seconds, before subsiding into a choking, bubbling, gargle. Every head in the crowd and on the stage turns towards Bridge Street and the river.

'I fear it may be Father!' cries Cicely, clutching at Anna's arm. They make for the church gate, but many are there before them.

Mr Kindred is propelled from his settle by the sudden noise. The figure is gone from his kitchen bench, and the yard is empty, the wooden door swinging in a gentle breeze. There are sounds of a wrenching and a struggle behind the fence. Josiah is not a brave or a foolish man, and is about to retreat inside and bar the door, when a portion of the fence collapses in the yard, revealing a huge black hound, with a stout rope around its neck, attached to a wooden stake, which it has just succeeded in pulling from the ground. The stake swings in an arc over the dog's back as it advances into the yard, head down and growling low in its throat.

'Excuse me, sir,' says a voice behind Josiah, 'if you would just step aside for one moment.'

Richard has never fought with a dog before. He has fended off fierce or snappy hounds in his time, but not one that appears intent only on killing him. Twice the dog lunges for his throat, the first time he gets in a cut on its shoulder, the second he feints as it passes and gives it a blow with the flat of his sword on its rump. The third time Richard drops to his knees and wrestles with the creature, keeping its head and fearsome jaws above his shoulder. It is now that he feels the awful strength of the beast, as it digs in its back legs and forces him to the wall. He quickly releases his hold and twists back into the open yard, cutting the giant dog again on the back. But the creature is both nimble and quick witted. It drives in at Richard's waist, and as he makes to parry, it bites up and to the left, catching him by the wrist. His sword flies away across the yard and the dog is on him, knocking him into the dust. Richard pulls out his dagger and jabs for the dog's throat, his blade breaking on its breastbone. He scrabbles to his feet and backs into the Kindred's henhouse, up against the house wall, holding the broken dagger in his left hand. The dog bares its teeth and prepares to spring. There is a gentle thump beside the captain. A small, dark furry shape drops onto the henhouse roof, glances briefly at Richard. and hops down into the yard. It jumps up into the astonished dog's face, down between his legs and out towards the gate. The dog turns and gives chase, and Richard uses the precious seconds to retrieve his sword. He runs to the gate in time to see the creature jump right into the river, followed by the dog. It as if a mighty swell or whirlpool arises, washing the shallow banks, and legs and jaws and great furry backs rise and fall in the foaming water. Then there is peace, and a still dark shape drifting off down the middle of the river.

The captain begins to be aware that his right arm is weightless, and that he is covered in blood. A restful sleep, right here by the river, seems an excellent notion, as he topples headlong into the reeds.

'Steeped in gore, he was!' says Thomas Rune. 'Bleeding from divers wounds, and half-drownded!'

'There are only three, as it happens,' said Doctor Gordon, 'his wrist, a cut on his knee, and a slight contusion on his cheek. But had he fallen five feet to the south he would have imbibed several pints of the Waveney, and may have been full drownded.'

'But what a hero!' says Thomas. 'Vanquished the ghost dog of Bongay and saved the life of an eminent feoffee!'

Richard opens his eyes. He is lying on a couch in a strange house, and a kindly looking woman is wiping his brow with a warm cloth. She looks vaguely familiar. He sits bolt upright.

'Did you see its eyes?' says Richard.

'You are to keep your arm still,' says Doctor Gordon, 'if you wish your fingers on that hand to keep your commands you must allow the sinews to mend. Drink this.'

He proffers a small cup, which Richard drains and gags upon.

'My own concoction,' says the doctor proudly, standing back as Richard slumps back on his couch. 'A few herbs and essences, mixed with the juice of some distilled sloes. It is an aid to rest and repose.'

'It's an aid to unconsciousness, certainly,' murmurs John Kettle, lifting the captain's eyelid. 'His tabula hath been well and truly rasa'd.'

Richard is asleep on a white sandy shore. He doesn't care anymore, about anything.

He wants the sea to come and cover him. Whenever the waves come close someone or something appears and drags him a little up the beach. There is a woman, who groans and struggles with his heaviness; there is a giant, bristly hog, who gently nudges him away from the water with its snout; there is a great black, red-eyed hound, which grabs his collar in its teeth and drags him growling from the waterline, and there is another woman, who cradles his head in her lap, and says if he must die then that is up to him, but it seems a poor return for just a scratched wrist and a bump on what is already quite a "bumped" head, and what, with him saving her father from certain death, she might begin to consider forgiving him for his assumptions about her regarding Master Belwood, and even to entertain seeing him at some future date with a regard to renewing their intimacy – if such was his wish.

EIGHTEEN

It is a bright blue-sky day in Bongay. After church many of the people are to be found in the town square. There are three rumours circulating this fine Sunday morning. The first is that Captain Brightwell has suffered terrible injury and probable death by an encounter with Black Shuck, the ghost dog lately seen at St Mary's Church; the second that Mr Josiah Kindred, of Bridge Street has received such an affright in the aforesaid assault that his hair has turned pure white; and the third that Mr Belwood is somehow implicated in the proceedings.

Mrs S declares that as soon as she entered the upper room of The Fleece on the day of her interview, she could see death in the captain's eyes. Mrs W said that men with red hair very often die in September, and Mrs T is of the opinion that asking after Shuck brings you to his attention, and your certain demise, as has certainly befallen the poor captain. The "poor captain" is sitting in Doctor Gordon's garden, on a pallet next to Mr Edmond Denny. Medically, they have met at a sort of crossroads; Richard from rude health to a painful but not life-threatening arm injury, and Edmond from the shady, sunken lane of near death to the high road of near-recovery.

'It'll be like a Second Coming!' says Edmond.

'How so?' says Richard.

'Well, you can be sure you have died and been buried several times over out there in the square this morning; so any subsequent signs of life will surely be seen as another form of miracle.'

'Perhaps we can reappear together,' says Richard, 'and our resurrection will so shock the townsfolk that they may forget the Black Dog altogether for a few moments?'

'I for one would not care to hear or see of it again,' says Mr Kindred, who is also reclining on a bench in the garden. Miss Kindred is sitting beside him, stroking his pure white hair.

'However, it must make your report to the bishop a little easier, now that the creature is no more?'

'Only a very little,' sighs Richard, trying to picture that prelate's austere and increasingly puzzled expression as the tale of wild chickens, phantom dogs and killer rabbits unfolds before him. 'I'll need John Kettle and Humfry with me, or he'll think I've made it all up or lost my wits, or both.'

Miss Kindred covers her mouth, almost spluttering with laughter.

I've said something amusing! thought Richard. I have made her laugh! Laughter lights up her whole face. She has laughed at him before, but more for his strange behaviour than his wit. It is a relief to say something in front of her and not appear a great fool. This was a puzzle he had spoken about to John Kettle.

'Why is it, that with the aid of God's providence we are – some of us – and here I exempt Mr Belwood and the Reverend Fleming – blessed with the gift of wit and winning ways, such as can charm a very fence-post from the ground, and yet when we wish to use this weapon in the way for which it was surely intended, to make ourselves pleasing to young women, we – I – cannot form a single phrase out of my dry mouth that does not make me seem a great dolt or a preening ninny?'

'I think it is the divine signal that there is deep feeling between you,' says John Kettle. 'The less you can utter, the more it means.'

'But how then will anything ever get said?' says Richard.

'You are the living proof of my theorem!' says John. 'Recall when you thought Miss Kindred was besotted of Master Belwood, your words were as sharp and wintry as a February frost. And now you know again what everyone else knew all along, that she cares nothing for him, you can barely look at her without leaving your mouth hanging open! Do you think she cannot see this? That she needs words to confirm it?'

John Kettle is not only an excellent scribe, but also an astute observer of human nature. If he were to publish a pamphlet on "The Principles of Good Courtship", it would surely run to several editions, and help to make his fortune.

I know what you're going to ask: our little group of friends are recovering together in the sunshine, the town square is awash with gossip and rumour, but where are those other interesting characters, the Black Dog Brotherhood? Well (and this is one in the eye for all those of you who say the world is just random chaos, and that there is no plan or fate for any of us), they are all at the same time leaving the town by different points of the compass.

Mr Strine has abruptly tired of running a hostelry, and has decamped in a southerly direction, to stay with his sister in Halesworth. The ill-favoured pot-boy is his unwilling companion, and it is he who is laden with most of Mr Strine's goods and chattels. As has been mentioned, the weather is fine in Bongay this morning, but a fierce black rain squall sweeps across the Ilketshalls at about this time, soaking Mr Strine and his pot-boy to the bone.

Mr Vyner is also very wet, but that is because he is in the river, bobbing along towards the eastern coast and the sea out beyond the Ropewalk Beck and Wainford Mill, well on his way to Beccles. He utters not a word of complaint as he floats along, as he is quite dead and drowned, and is more of the river than on it. When he is found, washed up in the meadow below Puddingmoor, his hair is as white as Josiah Kindred's, but he carries no wounds on his body.

And here is the Reverend Abram Fleming, on a small pony, huffing and puffing his way westwards past Earsham. There is a stiff breeze blowing, and he frequently stops and looks back on the dusty white road. He has had his fill of market towns and the countryside, and has resolved never to leave London again. What is that, over there, among the trees? It is only some cows, settling down with their backs to the wind. Brown and white cows. Or is one of them black? No, there are no black cows in this part of the country, that mad farmer friend of Belwood's had said as much. Anyway, what else could it be? The dog was dead and gone in the river, and with it the Brotherhood, and a goodly part of his income. Who was going to buy a pamphlet about a Ghost Dog sent as God's wrath and retribution, and now found rent and drowned in the river? Damn Bongay and all dogs! The black cow raised its head, stood up on its legs and began trotting up the field, towards the road, in a most un-cow-like manner.

Abram, resolving to look no more on the local flora and fauna, pulls his hat down over his eyes, claps his heels to the indolent pony, and makes haste for Diss.

That leaves Mr Thomas Belwood, who has also been gripped by an overwhelming desire to leave this town. He has no very clear idea of where he is going, but he has heard enough from the inane ramblings of Sara, his servant girl, and the shouts and calls outside in the street to know that he has been somehow implicated in the recent exciting and murderous events.

'Oh yes,' said Sara, 'the whole town is in an uproar with you, sir! It seems they think you have something to do with this terrible dog business. I said that couldn't possibly be you, being you're a gentleman and everything, and a person of quality, and that would all be made clear by you and the Reverend gentleman as soon as could be explained. Where is he? Oh, he left over an hour back! He was in a tearing great hurry too! Well, that's your bag packed as you asked, sir, there's a pasty and a flask of ale in the saddle bag, now I must beg leave of half an hour, as I am summoned to Captain Brightwell on this "dog" business, if I can be spared?'

Mr Belwood clenched and unclenched his fists but could find no speech. One more murder would make no difference now. They could only hang him the once. He would be doing the town a service, and might even be remembered with fondness for a final selfless act. But Mr Belwood was a man of a certain fastidiousness, who preferred others to play out his violent wishes, so he merely said, 'Begone, woman!' as he rushed to the stables.

The horse seems unwilling to stir herself, and refuses to hurry, so Mr Belwood has to almost drag her through the yard, across Earsham Street and down St Edmund's Lane towards the common. Mr Belwood has not been on the common for years, since he was a boy, but he knows there is a plank bridge over on the Ditchingham side of the river. He points the mare in a north-easterly direction, but a thick mist has now descended about him, and he soon loses the path. After ten minutes of trotting, they are brought up short by the river. But where upon the river? Mr Belwood peers across the water, looking for a landmark on the far shore. While he is staring so hard and seeing nothing he drops the reins for an instant and the mare is off, trotting back to her stables.

A general animal curse, only slightly muffled by the mist, rings through the morning air, damning to hellfire and perdition all mares, horses, dogs and pigs. Had Mr Belwood been present in Bridge Street the previous evening, he would surely have added black rabbits to this list of the accursed.

If the Reverend Fleming had been present, instead of urging his pony westwards, he might have felt it incumbent upon him to point out the pointlessness of cursing dumb animals, as they were not deemed to be worthy of possessing souls, so could have no interest whether they were in purgatory, perdition, hell or heaven. (The Reverend Fleming might here have reflected on the teaching of Ecclesiastes, about there being a time and a place for everything; because if he had made a remark like that, at this time, in that place, it would surely have got him flung in the river.)

His cursing and stamping over, reason returns briefly to Mr Belwood's throne. If he is, as he must be, on the south bank of the river, he has only to proceed to his right, and he will eventually come upon the wooden bridge! His countenance is kept up by this thought for a few minutes, until the path begins to wander back southwards, skirting a copse of trees.

Mr Belwood finds himself in a shallow reed bed. He is lost again. The mist has grown thicker. He takes three steps backwards and his feet are upon firm ground once more. There is the sound of twigs snapping. It can only be some field hand or shepherd out here so far from the town. At least the dolt will be able to direct him to the bridge. Mr Belwood pulls his hat down over his eyes and prepares to greet his rescuer. Here he comes, now, quickly along the path, almost running to meet…

NINETEEN

'There was not a mark upon his face or body,' says Richard to the bishop, as they sat once more in his sunny, walled garden. 'The mist cleared as quick as it had come, and the maid said he had been gone but an hour, and his horse no more than a half. Doctor Gordon said he looked like a man who had died of fright, and had certainly been stricken with some seizure, but could give no definite cause.'

'Well, I wish death on no man,' says the bishop, 'but Mr Belwood might be said to have by his deeds wished it upon himself! It was a just and richly deserved end, by whatever manner! What news of the wayward cleric, Fleming?'

'Fled back to London, as far as can be told,' says Richard. 'He has vowed never to venture into these "barbarous lands" again, according to his latest pamphlet. We have been given up to the "banshies and the bishop", as he winningly puts it.'

'A great relief,' says the bishop. 'Let us hope he holds fast to his resolution! And the other miscreant, Costerden?'

'He was apprehended on the road to Bury. He would say nothing to his captors until he learnt of Mr Belwood's demise, whenceforth he crowed like a Ditchingham chicken, and was very keen to tell us all he knew in return for some lesser punishment. It seems Mr Belwood had laid plans with a number of the feoffees to increase their property and influence at the expense of other men of means in the town. There is a law in Bongay that once the number of feoffees falls to eight, either by death or removal, another sixteen must be chosen, and Belwood had a number of his toadies and cronies ready and willing to fill these places in return for handouts and favours. Before the storm, there were just eleven remaining, two of whom were Adam Fuller and John Walker. Belwood had planned to strangle them in the belfry, and had Vyner and Costerden carry out the deed, only for the tower to be struck that day with a thunderbolt. The dog was released deliberately into the church to kill Mr Kindred, but he did not attend church that morning, due to an attack of ague, brought on by a long evening in The Chequers. Costerden and Vyner threw the bodies of Fuller and Walker into the base of the tower, and left them in the nave during the melee of the storm, so it would look as if the dog had slain them. The Stares boy, who has no wits, had wandered from his pew into that in which Mr Kindred usually sat.

Costerden had placed an old glove of Kindred's under the seat, which the dog had been trained to seek out.'

'So Mr Kindred was saved from a savage death by a sore head!' says the bishop.

'Yes, but the poor Stares boy received his griping for him. When Belwood found out only two of the three were dead he lost no time in exhorting the Reverend Fleming to produce his pamphlet, so it would look as if the attacks were supernatural. He knew the old legend of the Bigod's dog and of Black Shuck, and thought he could use his killer dog in this guise, to further reduce the number of honest, upstanding feoffees.'

'A dark design in which he almost succeeded!' says the bishop.

'He could be said to have brought about his own downfall,' says Richard. 'He knew the Black Dog of legend had not been seen in the town in thirty years, so felt secure in reviving the ghost to suit his own ends. But it seems he was too successful. Black Shuck is thought to be a "Shilly-Shally", to use the local expression, an animal that can change shape at will. One of the defences against it is that it can be kept secure if imprisoned while in benign form, or not that of a giant ravenous dog. There was a persistent rumour in Bongay that it was last seen in King Henry's time, in the shape of a dark lady, who had been walled into a chamber, but no one knew, or would say where. It is my belief, and that of the town reeve and of Mr Edmond Denny that this spirit, shape, call it what you will, was released by animadvert from its prison when Mr Belwood, while excavating for a window to his own vanity, ordered the blocked door to be opened in pursuance of his own greed. And that it became very active for a time, and seen by many in different forms, and acting specifically against the interests of Mr Belwood.'

The bishop is looking quizzical.

'I saw the face of a woman etched on that chamber wall,' says Richard, 'as did Augustyn, whom you know cannot say so. I saw and heard two great hounds fighting before me in a dark cellar, one of whom vanished into nothing. My very life was saved by a small black rabbit, which turned into some great subterranean beast, which drowned and made an end of Belwood's dog. I do not know what any of these things mean, but I do know and swear that I witnessed them.'

'So how do you think Mr Belwood met his end?' says the bishop.

'I do not know for certain,' says Richard. 'I think he may have met something out on that common which – Humfry puts this best – which "realised all his fears"!'

'Well,' says the bishop, 'write me a report, detailing all Mr Belwood and friends' nefarious activities, but leave out all the supernatural stuff, or you'll have every witch and necromancer in Norfolk chanting and hooting at your door. So, is Bongay now a quiet hamlet once more, such as is safe for a prelate to pass through?'

'They still cling to their dog,' says Richard. 'They have already named a lane and an alehouse after it. As for a quiet hamlet, these country places are not half as sleepy as we would think them!'

'John Kettle mentioned a play and a football game, among other things,' says the bishop.

'John Kettle has been a most trusted companion, whom I would always have by me on any like exploit. And Humfry smoothes the way in all circumstances.'

'I was going to ask what you have done with your "protector"?' says the bishop. 'You cannot have mislaid him?'

'Augustyn has signed to me to ask you if he might remain with Mr Mellendyne at The Fleece Inn for the nonce. Mr Mellendyne has taken a great liking to him, and Augustyn serves him well as a cellar-man, keeper of the peace and companion at games.'

'I am happy to oblige,' says the bishop. 'It is always good when someone who is a misfit to the world finds a home and is at peace. Will you – er – tell him yourself?'

'I had – I have plans to return to Bongay tomorrow, to tie up any loose ends, and to pay my respects to Lady Sherborne, and the doctor, and call in on Mr Denny of course, and—'

'It would be good of you also to see those feoffees that held true during recent times,' says the bishop, rising and shaking Richard warmly by the hand, 'especially Mr Josiah Kindred – and his family? If you are passing that way? Here, I have a book for you to give him!'

'Thank you, My Lord,' says Richard. 'I will surely find the time to deliver your gracious gift.'

'Hmm,' murmurs the bishop, 'John Kettle said just now it was you who would soon be receiving a "great gift". What could he have meant by that?'

TWENTY

So, it is "goodbye" then. I know – we just feel we're getting to know and like some of these people, and have begun asking after them, but it really is time to go. They have done what they set out to do, and there is really nothing left to tell. It's time to let them get on with the rest of their lives… and we with ours.

Or, if you must…

Augustyn sits on a bench by a sunny wall in the backyard of The Fleece, eyes closed and resting from his exertions in the cellar. Mr Mellendyne and Miss Poope idly toss quoits and pass the town gossip between them. Of which there is little of late, although Anna is sure Mrs Kindred said something about the captain paying a visit again sometime soon…

John Kettle pulls down the rusty latch on his window and opens it onto the sunlit Norwich street. He takes a deep breath, sings a small snatch of "The Ballad of Robin Hood", picks up his quill and delves again into his *History of English Dialects*; this morning's puzzle being why the people of the south who live around Portsmouth and Southampton do not seem to have an 'h' to spare among them in their speech, while the denizens of Dorset and district seem to want to add one to every other word in their vocabulary…

Humfry Trip has been given a whole day off, so is thinking of nothing other than an extended dinner hour in The Adam and Eve, catching up with the city life, watching out for any comment from the landlord about black dogs, at which point he will offer to tell them – just fill my glass first – of the strange and terrible, but true tale of the Black Dog of Bongay. Humfry has not had to buy a glass of his own ale in a week…

Richard has left Poringland and Woodton and is nearing the crossing at Ditchingham, when he happens upon Mellchioedech Foweler, strolling along the dusty road, with a large basket of eggs on his arm.

'Good day to you, Cap'n!' says Mr Fowler. 'We didn't look to see you again, so soon! There's not been another surfeit of ghost dogs I ain't been told about?'

'No, I assure you, I've come simply to visit the feoffees who stayed true to the town and pass on the bishop's thanks, and see after Mr Denny, and perhaps look in on Mr Kindred—'

'*Mr* Kindred?' says Mellchioedech, shading his eyes with his hand as he looks up at the captain. 'Well, I'm sure he'll be very pleased at your concern, and I can tell you Edmond is very much mended, and that she is as bonny as ever she was – oh, though of course it's her father you say you've come to see. Well, I'll now be on my way, these eggs won't walk by themselves to the Manor! I ha' just fed the chooks, so they'll be all over the crossing, just you step your horse around them, and they won't be no bother.'

"She is as bonny as ever she was." John Kettle would approve of the brevity, clarity and the truth of this sentiment, and note the phrase in his dictionary. Richard rides on, and carefully walks his horse around the circle of feeding chickens. "She is as bonny as ever she was." A tendril of light brown hair tucked behind her ear, which fell forward again when she cradled his head. How many black dogs would he wrestle to have his head cradled so again?

'Er – Captain? Is that you?'

It is a woman's voice, from somewhere above. Richard looks up and spies a smiling Mrs Susan Curdye upon the bridge. He is in the river again.

'I thought that was you! Of course, you must please yourself, but the custom hereabouts is to go over bridges rather than under them. Look now you're all wet! I'm now going up the street to see Mrs Kindred and Cicely for an hour, do you come with me and dry those boots and things?'

As Richard leads his horse from the water he looks back at the sea of white chickens on the mound and spots, there in the middle, a pair of furry black ears. One ear bends, then the other, then they are gone.

'Did you see?' he says to Susan Curdye, but she is impatient to get him home and dry.

'Come, Captain, before you catch yourself a chill, there'll be a warm fire waiting up the street. Now, my Bernard was saying, only this morning…'

Matador

For exclusive discounts on Matador titles,
sign up to our occasional newsletter at
troubador.co.uk/bookshop